Angelic BLOOD

A Blood Novel

TAMARA ROSE BLODGETT

ANGELIC BLOOD
Book Five: The Blood Series
Copyright © 2015 Tamara Rose Blodgett

ISBN-10: 1503008819
EAN-13: 9781503008816

Cover Design: Claudia McKinney
Editing suggestions provided by Red Adept Editing

Praise for **THE BLOOD SERIES**….

"…. This book had everything, action, mystery, adventure, strong characters, friendship and love. Once in a while you come across a book that touches you emotionally, Blood Singers is just such a book…"- *Beth tometender.blogspot.com*

"…I love that Blodgett keeps the reader guessing who Julia will end up with throughout the entire novel: William, the kind, compassionate vampire that shares her blood and truly cares for her…Jason, her husband turned feral by the unforgiving weres, or Scott, her destined mate according to the Blood singers…only time will tell~" *Shana of AbookVacation.com*

"…I have three different series of books by this author, and all of them are outstanding, deserve best seller status. She puts everything in her books you could want: intelligence, humor, romance, family, adventure, suspense, action, etc. etc…" *-di1949*

"…This series is one of the best I've read and this is the best book in the series so far. There is so much going on. I love the fast pace and all the action…"- *Mellissa*

Dedication

Elias Carter Blodgett

You don't know it yet, but you changed my life….

Character Index:

Blood Singers/talent:

Julia- Queen of the Singers; Telekinetic/telepath
Scott- Royal Singer Blood; Deflector/Combatant
Brendan- Tracker/pyro
Michael- Illusionist
Jen- Telekinetic
Cyrus- Healer
Paul- Negator/amplifier
Angela- Feeler
Marcus- Region One
Jacqueline- Royal Singer Blood; Region Two Leader
Victor- Region Two/Combatant- Boiler/Flame of Blood
Lucius- Combatant
Cynthia "Cyn" Adams - Rogue/Healer
Heidi- Reader
Trevor- Deflector

Northwestern Were Pack:

Lawrence-Packmaster
Emmanuel "Manny" - Beta to Lawrence
Anthony "Tony" Daniel Laurent- Second to Lawrence
Adrianna "Adi"- Alpha female

Southeastern Were Pack:

David- Packmaster
Alan Greene- Alpha male
Lacey Greene – female Were and Alan's sister
Buck "Slash"- Alpha male
Karl Truman- former Homer detective
Ford- Alpha male/ FBI agent
Reagan - Moon Warrior, Lacey's daughter

Southeastern Vampire Kiss:

Merlin- Coven leader (now deceased)
William- new coven leader (now deceased)
Brynn- New leader of the Southeastern

Northwestern Vampire Kiss:

Gabriel- Coven Leader
Claire- William's cousin
William- Runner/shifter/Singer blood

Unseelie Sidhe fey:

Queen Darcel- Sidhe
Tharell- mixed Sidhe warrior
Cormack- Sidhe warrior
Domiatri "Domi"- Sidhe warrior
Rex- Sidhe
Kiel (*key-ale*)- dragon shifting Sidhe
Celesta- Sidhe warrior
Delilah - Vampire, third to Julia, Scott's half-sister

Rogue Reds:

Ezekiel "Zeke"

Rogue Alpha female Were:

Tessa

FEDS:

Tom Harriet
Tai (*tie*) Simon

Western Were Pack:

Tramack
[the] **Lanarre:**
Drek
Bowen
Taliah

1

"**J**ules!" Jason screams, sliding toward her like a runner at home base.

Julia looks up at him, holding her guts inside her body. "Oh, God—no!"

Jacqueline rises from behind Julia's torso, where she'd lain to avoid Tharell's body.

She wears Julia's blood.

"Looks like someone has lost their head," Slash comments dryly, stepping over Tharell's body. His humor leaks away when his eyes catch sight of Julia.

"Julia—what can we do?" Jacqueline asks, ignoring everything else.

A demonic blurs past them, its tail sailing into the head of a Singer with well-practiced precision. Julia's veins flash golden at its nearness.

"Fuck!" Jason rages, leaping to his feet as he puts his back to her protectively.

"Cyn," Julia croaks.

Jason whirls around, understanding blooming on his features.

I need Cyn.

He nods, peering into the thick of the battle. "I can't see her!" he shouts then sprints into the fray. Julia fights to remain awake, but her eyes feel buggy in their sockets, too wide and dry. The pain sharpens her senses, helping her stay alert—and alive.

A bubble of blood forms from her lips, and Julia feels herself beginning to slip. She's still mortal, still vulnerable—and so very tired.

Her eyes meet Jacqueline's. Julia sees the knowledge of her death reflected in them. Julia holds herself in position, avoiding Tharell's head, which was no longer attached to his body, beside her.

I can hold on a little longer. Julia closes her eyes and concentrates on her breathing.

In.

Out.

"Jacqueline," Domi says from behind Julia.

Julia cracks open her eyelids, and Jacqueline stills, her eyes growing wide. The demonic rushing toward them is gaining momentum. Julia is vulnerable and wounded—vulnerable to *true death*, as William would call it.

Julia's eyes bulge, and she licks dry lips.

The blood bubble on her lips pops with a soft smack, and she not dare move her hands from where her organs pulsate beneath her fingertips.

Domi turns casually, clotheslines the devil's warrior, and crushes the red flesh around the demonic's windpipe.

As the demonic folds to his knees, the saber in Domi's hand flashes downward, cutting the head from the soldier of their mutual enemy.

The twang of swords and weaponry is the dark orchestra that plays for them.

Jacqueline's mouth hangs slack as she turns slowly to look at Domi, then at the demon lying still at his feet. Finally, her eyes come to rest on Tharell.

Julia knew of Tharell's comprehensive duplicity against Domi, but there Domiatri stands in emerald splendor, proud and tall. His throat is bisected by a rope-like scar. He steps over the demon, shooting an indifferent glance at Tharell's body before he faces Jacqueline.

Julia swallows her groan—her hands are drenched with her own blood.

"Domiatri," Jacqueline breathes in shock as Slash picks up the sword that the castrated Tony let drop.

"Nice work on the devil," Slash says casually. But there is nothing casual about his restless gaze as it travels the field, looking for other demonics. He seems resolved to protect her until Jason can get back.

Julia clenches her eyes shut. *Where is Jason?* Only Cyn can fix the mess of her body.

Slash toes Tony's corpse, and Julia breathes against the pain in her gut. The sounds of men striking each other is like listening to slabs of meat being tenderized.

Julia's stomach roils against the metallic fragrance of blood and death in the air and the sounds of flesh succumbing to fists and blade. Her limbs grow numb as her vision narrows to gray edges and a black center.

Julia drags in raw breaths.

Domi scoops Jacqueline against him. "Tharell thought to murder me."

"I know," she replies.

Julia's skin begins to pulse golden-silver, shining like a beacon as one of the demonic approaches.

She tries to roll away and can't manage it.

It hisses, driving its tail toward her as blood pumps out of her body, but Slash turns, catching the end of the whipping rope-like appendage with the borrowed saber and cutting it off. The deep-red stalk fishtails sickly and falls. Inky blood spurts out of the amputated stump as the demonic shrieks.

Jacqueline sinks to her haunches beside Julia as Domi swings his own sword and takes off the horned head. A warm hand covers her own blood-slicked ones.

The sudden silence that falls is peaceful and heavy, like scarlet snow that never lands. The demonic are losing the battle, and the shine of Julia's skin dulls as the second demon's life ebbs as it lies a few feet from her in a pool of black blood.

Julia knows with perfect certainty that she doesn't want to die in this thankless field of war and death.

The salt of Jacqueline's anguish splashes on Julia's face. Gasping her last breaths, Julia watches it all as though she's no longer in her own body.

Out of the corner of her eye, Jason emerges like an oasis in the midst of a forever desert. Cyn is wound tightly around his back as he dives between the last brandishing fists. Blood arcs, spattering them as they charge between the opposing forces.

"Do not go, Julia. Your people need you," Jacqueline says, rubbing Julia's icy hands as though the motion will repair her. More unshed tears fill her dark eyes, which are so like Scott's.

"I do, as well," she adds in a whisper.

Jacqueline, her enemy no longer, clutches Julia's hands while her fey lover fights off the remaining demonic behind them.

Jason lurches beside her, his wolfen form casting a shadow over her, and dumps Cyn at Julia's side.

Cyn's eyes widen in horror at what Julia assumes is the mess of her body. "Jules…oh, God—*no*."

Julia closes her eyes and Cyn's presence is a salve to her body, but not her words.

"I don't know if I can fix this," Cyn despairs.

Julia's eyes open to painful slits while Cyn's gaze roves her body. Julia's hope flees when she sees those expressive eyes.

The saber christened with demonic blood is going to slam dunk Julia into death. Tears riot down her face. Jacqueline holds one of Julia's hands while the other is in Jason's tight grip.

"Come on, Cyn. We haven't come all this way to back out now."

Cyn drags her finger underneath both eyes, swiping and flinging tears away. She inhales deeply and replaces Jacqueline's hands with her own. With a sigh, Julia lets hers slip apart, and they fall onto the grass. The air is cold compared to the heat of her injury.

"Oh, Jason." Cyn's voice trembles, sounding mournful.

"Don't you fucking die on me, Jules," Jason commands fiercely.

Julia doesn't promise anything—or even speak—because glorious warmth floods her stomach and spreads, leaking through her body like a bath of fire. She feels as though her body is melting into the grass, though the clangs and charge of battle still grow.

Nothing is more silent than death.

"That's it, Cyn!" Jason sounds desperate.

Julia relinquishes her ownership of this life, which was always a gift, not something she could expect to always have.

If she's the Rare One, she'll get through this. If she's not, Julia is convinced she was never meant to be anything to anyone. Julia's exhausted to her marrow.

She wants so much more from this life. She knows she has a sister somewhere in the Red Den of Alaska, and Julia wants Jason as a woman wants a husband.

More, Julia wants to actually live, not merely survive from one catastrophe to another. Like a candle flame in jeopardy of being blown out, she feels her soul flutter with indecision. Julia's will to live hangs in the balance.

"*No*—Jules. Help me here!" Cyn screams.

Julia's eyes flutter open to find her people quietly gathered.

"The demonic?" Julia chokes out, her eyes frantically searching for the deep-crimson bodies, black horns, tails, and the soulless eyes.

None still stand. Their dead bodies litter the ground at her peoples' feet, and the Singers' skin doesn't shine. The beautiful veining that surfaced before and during the battle was nothing more than a warning of their mortal enemies proximity.

Cyn's hands clench over the wounds, and Julia's body arches against the grass as she gasps. Life fills her body where death sought to claim her. A thread of warmth runs to her fingers and toes. Her eyes sharpen, and her heart begins to beat a strong rhythm again. She rises up on her elbows, Jason's large hand at her back, and glances down at her belly.

Dried blood flakes on a deep scar that turns pink as she watches. Jason's eyes meet hers over the knitting wound. He puts his knees behind her back, and she leans back against him. His hands lock around hers, and he bows his head, unable to hold in the shuddering exhale of relief.

"Tony has failed." Domi's lip curls in satisfaction as he looks at Tony's body before moving on to Tharell's headless corpse. "Tharell failed, as well," he growls.

Slash gives a satisfied snort. "Still like how he lost his head." He gives Julia an apologetic glance, and Julia's lips turn up.

"It's okay, Slash." Julia doesn't miss Tony. His demise makes the earth a better place. Bright sunlight splashes over them, making Domi's deep-green flesh appear to sparkle with luminescence. It's somehow wrong to have a beautiful day as witness over this much death and bloodshed.

Jacqueline's eyes are round, shocked. Julia tries to sit up, but her core flinches at the motion.

"Julia—no way." Cyn's hands are splayed on her healing stomach, and Julia chokes up as Jason comes up behind, lifting as he stands with her cradled against his chest.

His body is covered with the light-red down of his wolfen form. The green discs of his eyes slow their spinning.

"The demon fuckers are gone." His voice sounds like falling gravel, making Julia flinch. "Our blood won out!"

Julia tips her head back against his shoulder, and he smiles, flashing rows of dangerous teeth.

Julia nods, still weak. "Where? How?"

With laser focus, Slash eyes Tharell's body with a consideration bordering on hate. "I say we pop Tharell's head back on and see if he can't tell us."

Julia shakes her head, ignoring the pain of yet another betrayal. "Too dangerous."

Slash pulls Adi from behind him, and she approaches Julia.

"This affects all of us now, Julia. We've won the battle, but not the war. The demonic left and ducked into their little fire hole or whatever. But they'll be back. We got a stay of execution because Tony dropped the ball…"

"Or balls," Cyn cackles behind her hand.

Julia smiles. Cyn's already recovering her sense of humor. If she were in Cyn's position, Julia didn't think she would be capable of laughing at anything.

"I say we stake him," Brynn says.

Julia blinks. The sun has sunk behind the trees, but the vampire stays in the shadows, offering his opinion safely out of the dangerous final rays of daylight.

Both Cyn and Jacqueline wear Julia's blood. As if she's made of glass, Jason carefully lowers Julia to the ground. Then Cyn's hands fall away from her body, revealing smooth unscarred skin, healed perfectly except for a black smear to the upper left of her belly button. It itches, but she's *alive*.

Julia inhales deeply, painfully, as she looks at the loss all around her. The casualties of her people fill the field.

But more bodies of the demonic lay testimony to the Singers' victory.

Her eyes come to rest on Tony last. His sightless eyes seem to gaze at her through a fog as if accusing her.

She tries to feel guilt or remorse, but she can't. This is the being who massacred nearly all the people of Region One. He raped Jacqueline and Lacey Greene. He was the horror that had plagued her and many others from the beginning, and now he's dead. Julia releases the breath she was holding, and the throbbing of her belly is her only physical distraction. She slowly lowers to her butt, exhausted.

Julia turns to Brynn, William's successor. "Stake Tharell?" she asks.

Domiatri comes into Julia's field of vision as Jason comes underneath her again, and she leans back against his knees. A knotted rope of scar tissue is a light-mint line across his neck. It appears to shine in the whitewashed daylight. Julia realizes it's healing before her eyes. The bumps integral to the scar tissue begin to smooth, and the shine begins to fade. Domi's skin rights itself in color, becoming grass green again where the pale-mint of the scar had bisected his throat. It's hard to look away.

"It will not be true death for Tharell until his body is burnt to ash."

All who are gathered look at Tharell, whose mouth is a gaping hole of silent screaming.

Julia backs away, and for the first time, she recognizes what she hadn't noticed before while pain rode her.

Tharell's alive.

She says the thing that damns any chance of her claiming to be the angel she supposedly is.

"Do it."

The men move forward to collect the pieces of Tharell, stepping over the fallen Tony as they do.

Tharell

Tharell's agony is so acute that he has no voice for it. No sound emanates from his ruined body to articulate his pain.

Domiatri has pinned his palms and feet to the ground with stakes a full foot in length. The agony of iron courses through his tortured body as it fights to heal the constant affliction of metal.

The scarred Were assists Domi in his torture as, for a fey as pure as Domi, touching iron ore would have been akin to handling acid.

Tharell understands he will reap what he has sown. Intellectually, he understands his part of the deceit. He did not want to do what he did. However, blood dictates all. Humans need it to live, and supernaturals are governed by its crimson pull.

A crude approximation of a reattachment of his head has Tharell's tendons and muscles stinging as they reassemble pathways severed by the decapitation.

However, the pain is nothing compared to the condemnation he receives from every quarter, every set of eyes set against him.

The blame is deserved, of course. None knew the black blood that flowed within his veins is master over all others because the angelic blood is dominant to those Singers who possess enough of it. Tharell closes his eyes in weary resignation.

A moment later, his face rockets backward with a slap, the sound of which fills the meadow. Though he does not cry out, Tharell groans from the worst physical misery of his life. A Sidhe warrior would rather die than admit weakness.

Tharell meets the dark gaze of the death bringer head on.

Of course they would use *him*, the strongest of all supernaturals.

The vampire Tharell had been a part of finding smiles down at him coldly. "Ah, to have a fey to torture," the vampire muses happily.

Tharell readies himself.

However, Julia is the one who comes to stand before him. His demonic blood riots in warning at the proximity of an angelic, especially one as pure as she is.

Natural-born enemies.

"Blooded Queen," Tharell manages from his healing throat and around the searing heat of his punctured palms and feet.

"You've been crucified," she says almost absently, though her eyes seem dull to any pleasure due to his pain.

He tries a nod and finds it unmanageable. "It appears that way." The irony of his physical positioning does not escape Tharell's notice.

Julia's golden hair is plaited, and many of the hairs have escaped the braid. Her eyes flash, and her veins, their power awoken to his ancestry, pulse like liquid gold and silver, mingling at the surface of her skin with every beat of her heart.

It is a standoff. Tharell knows Julia will want answers. And only he can decide their worth to him. He could always die again by her hand, to be resurrected again and again.

His immortality has proven to be his greatest weakness.

"I will confess the reasons for all my deeds for one thing in return."

Her eyes hold his in the bright light of the rising moon.

She gives a small despairing laugh. "Like you've got a bunch of options?"

Tharell has never seen so much grief in one gaze. He waits as the seconds pound by.

"What is it?" Julia finally asks with bald distrust.

"Kill me when I am through."

Julia stares at him for a full minute. She swipes at her face, flicking away a lone tear like a gem of resignation.

"Done," she says so softly that only the Were gathered nearby could have heard her.

Tharell hears her answer perfectly.

He begins to talk, knowing that a quick death by the Blooded Queen's mercy is better than the torture Praile would inflict upon him.

2

Julia

"*I* am a vessel," Tharell admits, grimacing. "We who possess the blood of the demonic all are."

Julia crosses her arms, wincing at her still-tender stomach. Cyn did a lot to alleviate the worst part of the wound, but when she gets closer to Tharell, Julia's mostly-healed injury flares like a lit match. She tries to dismiss the black smear that remains on her pale skin like an evil smudge. Its presence tugs at her subconscious.

She backs away, and the biting pulse lessens. "Don't lie."

As Tharell raises his head, the horrible scar like a streak of lavender lightning bulges across his throat, and Julia swallows her gorge.

"The fey do not lie, Blooded Queen."

"Oh, horseshit!" Cyn yells, tramping over to where he lays. She moves to her knees, careful not to soak them in the continuous seep of blood that courses out of the pads of Tharell's palms. "You lie by omission, you fucking grape. You made us believe there was some kind of treaty between the Singers and fey, and the entire time, you were just some lackey of the demonic, doing the plotting prick program."

Adi flashes a smile at Cyn. "Not to sound dumb, but who's your leader?"

"That's Michael's line," Julia says sadly, looking down to hide her tears. Jason puts his arm around her, and she looks up, way up into his changed face. His green eyes rotate slowly, and though it's hard to ascribe human emotion to the partially changed, Julia thinks he looks sad.

None of the Were have changed back to human—that's too dangerous. Holding the wolfen form doesn't take the energy that full wolf form does. And the majority of Weres can't achieve full form unless the moon is full.

"Let's not take all day here," Truman says, dumping another demonic corpse on top of the others.

We've got a pile of demons. Julia shudders and squelches a bubble of laughter.

"We don't want to be caught with our drawers around our ankles, swapping spit and shit." Julia frowns at Truman's comment, though it's the truth. *Point for him.*

"It does not matter. You can kill me. Burn me to ash and sprinkle my essence in a swift-moving river to rid me from this place." Tharell's azure eyes latch on to Julia's, and she shivers in Jason's protective embrace. "But Praile *will* come for you. He will use whoever and whatever has the blood of his kind to serve him."

"I'm tired of this douche," Jason growls in his strange part-animal timbre.

"Why?" Domi asks suddenly.

"We do not have time for this, Domiatri," Jacqueline reminds him quietly.

"We don't have the time to kill his ass, either," Truman says thoughtfully. "We need to beat feet outta here."

"I can do it," Brynn offers.

Tharell gives him a neutral look.

Julia knows it'd be impossible for her to be as calm as Tharell appears if she were presented with certain torture and death. That composure speaks to the nature of Tharell's existence.

She pushes stray hairs out of her face, more for an excuse to do something than for neatness. "I promised I would," Julia says. Everyone looks at her, and she feels her face grow hot.

"He tried to kill Jolly Green over there," Jason says from above her. Domi frowns at Jason.

"Guys, let's not set up a testosterone palace," Cyn remarks, throwing her arms up. "We still kill grape-boy, but on our own timeline, Julia didn't say *when* she'd do him."

Julia flinches.

Ignoring her, Cyn goes on, "Let's get together the Singers who want to come back to Region One. The Tony threat is gone, because he got his weenie chopped off." She flashes a grin and lets out a manic chuckle. "A great trend to dissenting dudes."

Adi snickers, and Julia dumps her face into her hands. Cyn is alarmingly practical, and it's somehow not cool right now, with Tharell being staked and a bunch of dead demons piled up on a death hill. It's too gross to be real. Yet it is.

Singers need to be buried, and the rest need to get back home, or what's left of their home.

"Cyn," Julia says.

Cyn lifts her shoulders. "All right, I know the whole dick comment was a little over the top…"

"At least we know where ya stand," Truman says thoughtfully, shooting her a wary glance.

Adi laughs.

Julia looks between the two. "Enough. Thank you for healing me."

Cyn rolls her eyes. "Of course, doll. Like I wouldn't have?" Her palms flip out and away from her body. "Doy."

"But I need less sarcasm and more action."

Cyn huffs, crossing her arms. "I say leave the demons for the vultures—and wonderful Tony. That's better than that mongrel deserves. We get whatever Singers want to come back to the Region One stomping ground."

A tear races down Julia's face, and she gives it an angry rub. She has no time for grief. "I want to take stock of survivors."

Domi turns to her. "I can bury the dead."

Tharell clears his throat. Domi frowns.

Julia presses the heels of her hands in her eyes, hoping to erase the vision of everyone casually discussing things over Tharell's staked body.

But he's still there when she lets her hands fall. The bodies of the dead still cant in an unbalanced way in the center of a field that was awash with blood during daytime and is now black tar all around them.

"No way!" Adi says, looking from Tharell to Domi. "This guy—this guy is such a backstabber." She narrows her gaze at Tharell, whose expression remains neutral, despite the horrible pain he must be in.

"We need him for speed. To bury the dead." Domi admits.

Julia rolls her bottom lip between her teeth. It's so unfair. But she can't leave the dead Region Two Singers to have their bones picked clean by scavengers. She just can't reconcile that move, not with everything else.

"Can he be…" Julia puts a hand on her forehead, tired to the bone. "Can he be contained?" she finally asks.

Brynn steps forward as darkness swallows the daylight and the moon's brightness sharpens above them. The two mingle in a kiss of time, twilight bridging night and day, and a smolder plays over his skin.

"That's better," he says, looking around at the darkness, where the daylight still leeches at the edges of the field. "I can handle the fey."

Domi frowns. "What assurance do I have that you'll not make a try for my life or Jacqueline's?"

Her fingers tighten around Domi's forearm, and Julia's eyes go to Brynn's face. But it's blank, like William's could be, every feature outlined as if it were carved in bleached ivory.

Brynn's fangs elongate, shining like ready knives. "None."

"Ah, I don't know," Cyn says, her eyes following the fey-vamp verbal ping-pong match with interest. "Brynn might not be a team player, Jules."

"We can't do much better than this. He was William's guy, right?" Truman turns to Julia for confirmation.

"He was William's second from the Southeastern Kiss. There's no motivation for allegiance, really," she confesses.

Brynn gives her a look so weighted, she stops breathing.

"What?" Truman barks.

"No vampire would harm the Rare One." He looks at each one of them, and Julia fights to make out his eyes in the swelling darkness. "In fact, it's my belief that Praile of the demonic is not the only one making a bid for the top echelon of supernaturals." Brynn spreads his hands to the side.

All eyes move to Tharell. "Let me up, and I will help for as long as my life serves a purpose." His bright gaze moves to Julia. "And then you *will* kill me."

Julia shakes her head in vague denial and his crisp blue eyes narrow on her.

"It must be by your hand. You gave your word."

I can't do it.

Julia's throat constricts, her breaths squeezed like frozen gasps inside her throat.

Domi strides over to stand next to Tharell's prone position and jerks out each stake with a meaty, wrenching suck. Tharell's face tightens but not a sound emerges from his lips. Domi steps away, and Tharell stands without assistance. Holes fill with fresh, pale-lavender flesh, and his unearthly blue eyes blink slowly.

Julia clamps down on her emotions. There've been too many traumas in a short span of time. She'd almost been murdered, countless more Singers had died, and that meant the death of so many from the one place where she was beginning to feel as though she belonged.

She blinks, realizing her lashes are wet. Jason gives a few soft, comforting snuffles against her neck.

Everyone backs away from Tharell as though he has the Black Plague. His eyes meet each of theirs.

"I deserve your disdain." His voice is low and full of emotion. "But if Praile comes again, he can force me to do his bidding. He could compel anyone who has sufficient blood of the demonic. And the Red Were are not immune to being used by the Master's summons."

Truman harrumphs in disbelief.

Tharell lasers a look of pure certainty at Truman. "Believe that I lie—I care not. Why should I warn you? What does it gain me?"

"Why not?" Cyn says. "You're obviously a stand-up dude."

Tharell's brows cinch.

"Not," Adi adds with a smirk.

Domi and Brynn step forward. "We take care of the dead Singers and find the ones who still live and wish to accompany us back to One—and faerie."

Domi's and Tharell's eyes lock in a battle of unspoken words.

⌒

"Julia," Jacqueline calls.

Julia stops, Jason a shadow beside her.

"I wish to find Gallagher. Perhaps he survived the blow."

Her head bows, and Julia knows, as sure as she's standing there, that Jacqueline's guilt is all for Victor. His brother is wounded and possibly dead, and Victor still remains unaccounted for.

Jacqueline can't atone for all the bullshit of her past. But she has a right to try.

Julia sighs, knowing she can't do anything about the epic mess. But Gallagher would be an important addition to One, though his desertion would leave Two leaderless. However, since all of One is decimated, the whole of Two would be better off returning with Julia than trying to piece together the Swiss cheese of their region. Their regions are more protected if they stand together than if they are apart.

"Let's try to find him. And"—Julia's eyes meet hers, though in the thick of the night, she can barely see anything but the whites—"I want a head count of all the Singers who still live and whether they want to come with us or not." She adds, "Convince them."

Jacqueline smiles as though she has a secret.

Julia thinks Jacqueline is perfect for the job. Part of what made her Jacqueline still peeks out through all of the changes since her time within faerie.

"Jules?" Jason rubs the back of her neck, and she wants nothing more than to sink against him, revel in his closeness, and enjoy the fact that she didn't die today.

But she can't. She has a duty to her people—and maybe a sister she doesn't know. But the thought of finding a sibling is a faraway wish. They're all still in survival mode.

Not to mention Scott and Lucius. The list goes on. Julia doesn't have time for the pity party she wants to throw for herself.

The dead are being entombed by a corrupt fey. Though her people have been annihilated, her promise to faerie still stands.

She's hungry, tired, and still healing. She's also in charge.

Julia says none of what she's thinking. Instead, she walks after a weary and pregnant Jacqueline in search of the one Singer she believes can help her and whatever Singers they can convince to accompany her.

Julia's not sure she would come if she were in their shoes. Violence holds claim to her, and death follows.

Not a great combo for a long life.

3

Tessa

*T*essa drives until she's nearly out of gas.

A 1950s neon sign flashes from a few blocks away as she heads up highway 99.

Gas-Food, it blinks. Well, part of it blinks. The *G* is missing in the first word. It's creepy. Tessa is somehow reminded of the *Psycho* movie from the 1960s.

She was a whelp in those days. Sometimes, Tessa doesn't think the longevity of being a Were is all that hot—like now, when she's hungry, tired, and broke.

She'll have to steal soon. Tessa hates that routine.

Just because she can take from the humans doesn't mean it sits well with her.

The gravel crunches under soft tires that need air. Tessa squints. Dawn is rolling over the Olympic Mountains, wrapping them in the sherbet tangerine of daybreak.

She can't believe the place is open. She parks by the air pump. Swinging the door wide, she begins to exit the low-slung car. "Ah!" Tessa turns to pop the glove box and rummages around.

The air pressure gauge in hand, she measures each tire. She fills all four tires, her eyes ceaselessly scanning her surroundings. Things are quiet for the moment as the hush of dawn adds to the false stillness. Tessa suspects the quiet before life begins a new day, is present for another reason besides daybreak.

Standing, Tessa swings her long ebony braid over her shoulder and jams a hand in the front pocket of her jeans. She extracts a crumpled ten dollar bill. She opens her hand, where a fifty-cent piece glows. As she holds it, the flesh of her palm begins to burn as if she's waving her open hand over a candle flame. Turning, she sets it on top of the roof of the vintage Impala. Carefully, using only her fingertips, she flips it.

The coin has the year engraved on it: 1964.

Silver.

Figures. Tessa can't wait to pass it into the currency of America. She's amazed it didn't burn a hole through her jeans.

Silver is poison to her kind, but Alpha females have some immunity. If she'd been male, the silver would have behaved like a burning ember inside her pocket.

Maybe their immunity had something to do with the importance of young. Tessa is always partially immune to silver while in quarter-change form.

Female Were are not plentiful, hence, her nomadic lifestyle. As soon as Tessa came of age, her pack began a bidding war for the right to mate her.

Knowing they would fight over her like what they were—a pack of wolves—Tessa decided to split before they had the opportunity. Now she's been rogue for two decades.

She's killed more males that she wants to admit.

Still, they were all deserving of death. Most were rogue like she was. But that did not give them the right to force her to mate with them.

Tessa trusts no male.

She exhales in a harsh burst, blowing the tendrils of hair that escaped from her braid out of her face. She can't allow herself to think of her slain packmaster father. He would not have allowed the bidding war.

Sadness tightens her body.

He would have given his only daughter a choice.

Her pack had robbed her of her freedom, along with her grief over his death. Tessa didn't have the luxury of mourning her father. He'd been challenged as packmaster by the one male who presumed victory would kill two birds with one stone. Tramack believed he would rule… with Tessa at his side.

As though I could ever forgive my father's murderer.

Tessa touches the heels of her palms to her drenched eyelashes and breathes deeply until she calms herself from a memory that is twenty years old.

The pain never seems to lessen.

It could, if not for Tramack's endless pursuit. His scouts seek her incessantly. Tessa manages to stay out of their sight for two years at a maximum before they find her again.

She lowers her hands and stares at the gas pump without seeing it. Finally, she punches in the pre-paid amount at ten dollars and fifty cents. She slams the old-fashioned lever and begins to pump the gas, her All-Star bright-red sneaker resting on the concrete curb that holds the pumps.

The gas pump chimes really quickly when all you have is ten bucks. Too quickly.

Tessa sighs, slipping the nozzle back into the holder, and shoves the lever down. A light breeze lifts the small hairs on her forearms.

A bird cries a warning.

Tessa's head jerks up, and her nostrils flare. Tendrils of hair swirl around her face, obscuring her acute vision.

The tiny hairs that humans ignore as a warning to imminent danger rise at her nape.

She ignores nothing.

Tessa moves away from the pumps, her eyes scanning the pocketed shadows of forest that are everywhere the eye can see. The gas station's yellow fluorescents cast a sick glow on the sidewalk that creates an uninspired strip at the entrance.

She sucks in huge lungfuls of crisp mountain air, closing her eyes and isolating her senses to just those of scent.

Tessa holds herself still.

Layered and comprehensive, the smells of cedar and Douglas fir needles, rich earth, lichen, asphalt, humans, and small forest animals drift over the olfactory regions of her nose.

Tessa chuffs in little bursts of air then parts her lips, taking breath through both her nose and mouth simultaneously.

The radar of scent surges out like big ripples and pings out at the odor of the large animals—felines, elk, and mountain goat.

Beyond that, the Pacific Ocean cleanses her palate, and she exhales.

Inhaling more deeply, she holds the air inside her lungs, and on this exhale, she smells something out of place.

Mud.

Her eyelids flip open.

Two men exit the forest. Tessa takes their measure, her heartbeat ticking faster. Her nose flares frantically.

She smells only the mud.

Then she sees them clearly. Beyond the black border of the forest and in the first light of day, Tessa understands why she can't scent them. She would laugh if the situation weren't so dire.

The Were are covered in the mud of the tidelands. That was why the smell of the sea was so strong.

If she hadn't been so busy cataloging, she would have known the ocean shouldn't smell so close. Tessa had become complacent. She hadn't been thorough and got caught with her panties down.

"Hello, Tessa," says one of the two.

They're obviously guards.

Tessa slouches against the car, crossing her sneakered feet at the ankle.

"Hey, boys."

The one who spoke raises a brow. "We're glad we could get a chance to talk to you."

"I'd think my answer would be obvious by now. Or did the other two dogs I put down not let you know my thoughts on the subject?"

He scowls, casting a glance at the dumb pup all but wagging his tail beside him.

"Byron," he says, twirling a finger in the air. The quiet one moves wide, making it impossible for her to see them both straight on.

Dammit.

The handle of the car door is a foot away from her hand. Tessa's palm itches to touch it.

Or her palm itches because of the silver coin she held for a few seconds.

The silver coin!

Tessa's finger twitches. The Were who thinks he can just swoop in and take her notices.

"Clever camouflage." She says to distract him, but she means it. She had almost no warning. Birds were sometimes helpful.

Tessa frowns and glances up at the tree for just a moment, catching sight of a snow-white bird. Her frown deepens.

Strange. But Tessa doesn't have time to think about the bird. The two Weres are closing in.

Her gaze finds Byron, who is half her age, inching closer. She looks for anyone who can help her.

The human at the cash register glances outside.

Their eyes meet.

She hasn't paid.

Don't come out here, she screams inside her head. Of course, he doesn't listen.

About sixty-five and portly, he shuffles out. "Hey, miss?"

"Yes?" Tessa replies without taking her eyes off the Weres.

"You gonna pay?"

"Yup," she answers. But she's not a hundred percent on that.

Byron inches closer.

Talkative looks at the heavyset cashier and narrows his gaze on him.

Some people don't have any instincts of self-preservation. This human is definitely one of them.

The cashier's eyes widen. What he sees is a six-foot-three-inch man covered in mud. To Tessa, he reeks of rotting sea vegetation. A human at that distance would have only his sight.

And the Were is a pretty weird view.

"What's going on here?"

Oh boy.

"What's going on, human, is you're going to march your fat ass back into that dilapidated store and pretend you didn't see us." A cruel smile lights his face like an old-fashioned camera bulb exploding.

Tessa's pulse quickens, and Talkative's nostrils flare as his face briefly turns in her direction.

She's had calls that were closer, but not by much.

"Listen, you're on my property. She hasn't paid, and I'm not letting two thugs who don't know what the inside of a shower looks like get in the way of me getting gas money owed. Go pack sand."

Talkative growls, and his skin shifts like liquid. His bones morph into a melting candle wax of sloughing skin as his face changes into wolfen.

He shakes like a wet dog, scattering clumps of tideland mud, both dry and wet.

Tessa's eyes tighten in pain as she performs her own quarter-change from the sloppiness of her human form. She dropped it once she arrived at the gas station, letting her guard down.

Instantly her ears, nose, and eyes become *more*. More sights reach Tessa, who can now pick out seaweed as small as a thread clinging to the Were.

She can smell the soap he uses underneath the sea muck.

His wolfen gaze falls to her as if she's his prey. The slow spin of yellowed irises rotate faster as he believes his quarry is almost his.

The cashier takes a hard look at the shit going down and hightails it back inside the store.

Smart man.

Talkative turns to her, now seven feet of striated muscle in motion. A coat of nutmeg-colored hair covers every bit of him as his short snout lifts, snuffling a few times to gather more of Tessa's scent.

A bell jangles, and the man comes back out and cocks a shotgun.

Tessa intuits everything. Action. Consequence.

"No!" she screams.

She thought he'd agreed and retreated, finally seeing the potential for his death by their hands.

But he's a typical human. *Have gun, will kill.*

Talkative can't move fast enough. The buckshot does, riddling the Were like a seven-foot-tall slice of Swiss cheese.

Talkative slows but doesn't stop. He launches himself at the porky cashier and tears out the man's neck upon landing.

Blood shoots up like water from a broken fountain, and bloodlust momentarily distracts him.

Tessa's head snaps to the right as Byron rounds the gas pump island. She moves quickly, snapping her fingers up to the coin on the roof of her car. *I might only have one chance.*

In quarter-changed form, Tessa has increased senses, speed, and strength. She uses that now, when only the car's length separates her from Byron.

She sprints to the trunk as he's at the hood.

She launches the coin with everything she has, and her hand-eye coordination is perfect in her changed form.

The edge of the coin slams into the middle of his forehead, and he howls. Instinctively, Tessa slaps her hands over her ears.

The coin burrows, doing the work for her as his skin parts to the most abhorrent substance to a Were. Tessa watches his skin burn, the edges blackening and folding open like the petals of a dying flower.

She backs away as blood spills.

His brains are next, and the coin doesn't disappoint. Like a horrible flat missile, it keeps seeking its target. There's no great healing that can arrest its progress. Male Weres can't heal from silver damage.

"Oops," Tessa breathes out as the river of what was inside his skull flows down his face. She begins to back away. Someone suddenly grips her upper arms from behind.

Smelling rancid mud, she slams her head backward. She's almost six-feet tall in her quarter-change form, and she uses that height, hopping as she flings backward. Tessa headbutts Talkative.

He staggers backward and she runs.

Tessa slips in all the blood and falls on her ass so hard her teeth snap together. He lurches toward her, and she rolls to stand.

A snowy bird that looks like a dove but isn't glides down in a loose spiral. The bird is a spot of purity in the blood that covers the asphalt. Talons splay.

Tessa grips the asphalt. The congealed blood is thick under her short fingernails. She pushes off, trying to put distance between herself and Talkative.

The bird screeches, high and brilliant, above and forward of her position.

The talons are sharp and big in Tessa's vision as it swoops closer. She ducks, and the bird flows over her head, lifting the loose hairs on her head and missing her by inches.

The screaming tells Tessa it has found its mark.

She stumbles forward and glances over her shoulder.

The bird's white feathers are covered in blood, and it carries an eyeball hanging by a gruesome tail of sinew.

The bird caws, slinging the orb off its talon. It spins in the crisp morning air and lands with a thud on the pavement. Puke threatens, but right now, it's survival of the fittest.

Talkative grabs the bird's body, and it cries in alarm. Tessa rushes the Were, who tracks her with his one good eye.

The bird dips its beak and takes his other eye while he's distracted by Tessa's approach.

The Were lets go of the bird and drops to his knees, howling.

Tessa hurtles forward, knocking him down. She grits her teeth as she slams his head into the asphalt.

Once.

Twice—bone shatters.

Three times.

His brains spill onto the asphalt.

Tessa wrenches her head to the right and sees Byron lying in his own brains, motionless.

A sigh escapes her, and she stands, trying not to shake. Tessa moves to push hair out of her face, and a bit of skull clings to fingers, which are covered in sticky gore with bits of dirt and granules of asphalt. She gulps.

Her eyes avoid the bodies. Instead, Tessa looks for the bird—and sees a Were instead.

Barely out of welphood, she stands before Tessa as naked as the day she was born.

Breathe, Tessa.

The day simply can't get worse. "I'm Tessa."

"I am Tahlia."

"Are you—did you?" Tessa doesn't know what to say, and it's a damn miracle there aren't more witnesses. At least there's *that* miracle.

"Yes. I am a Wereshifter."

Tessa had heard the legends. She'd just never seen it in the flesh.

Or feather.

Tessa eyes skate over the gruesome wreckage then return to the naked Were.

"You saved me."

Tahlia nods. "Yes."

"Why?"

She smiles, and Tessa is struck by the girl's beauty. "I could scent their intent."

"You're naked."

"I am," she gestures to herself. With a little laugh, she adds, "I had to escape something in a hurry, so…"

"You can come with me," Tessa gestures to the car. "I'll change the plates out at the next larger city."

She blinks once, very slowly. "Thank you."

"I have clothes," Tessa says.

"Okay."

Tahlia is stoic the entire time.

"Do you remember what you do when you change?"

Tessa doesn't. Once in human form, most Were do not remember what occurred while they were in their animal forms.

She nods. "Every bit."

Her full, perfect lips tremble as she shivers slightly in the cool air.

"Come 'ere," Tessa says.

Tessa wraps her arms around the smaller girl. "It'll be okay," Tessa says.

"I know."

Tessa tries not to feel guilty about the lie she just told the vulnerable girl.

And she fails.

Slash

Slash maintains the rear of their morose little expedition with ease. The Singers and supernaturals alike, who have not seen their fair share of war, look the same: shell-shocked or just plain shocked.

The Homer cop turned Red, Karl Truman, trudges along like it's any other day. Fighting to right the wrong is all that sort of male appears to need.

The Rare One continues on at her husband's side, and he maintains his wolfen form, as all the Were do.

Many of the Singers needed more healing than the handful of Healers could attend to, and they remain in need of more healing, rest, and food. There won't be much of that for the next few hours, though.

Brynn is the only vampire who remains. He's a shifty fanged fuck if Slash is any judge. And Slash believes he's a fine judge.

Tom Harriet still lurks in parts unknown, and he will certainly make another try for the Rare One. Julia will not be safe until the threat of the Reds from the Alaska den is over.

And now the demonic threaten her, as well—the fey.

And as much as Slash is loathe to admit it—the Singers are angelic. Not all, but some. Those Singers who manifested the telltale veining that pulsed like liquid gold and silver have been duly cataloged. It appears that roughly one in three are "angelic."

The angelic Singers were more successful during the siege of the demonic, and more of them survived.

Slash holds in the sigh of disgust at the memory of the pyre and the thought of Tharell, like a dog on a chain, waiting impatiently for his demon master's return so he can bite the first Singer who is near.

Slash voted for Tharell's immediate death. Whatever answers the Sidhe can supply are outweighed by the need for the group's safety. Tharell is a loose cannon. It seems more prudent to put him down like the dog he's proven himself to be than to keep him around. And the Unseelie warriors have proven tremendously hard to kill.

Slash spares a glance at the green Sidhe, Domiatri. A thread of scar tissue remains at his throat. Slash guesses that after another day, even that will be gone. Slash didn't ask how he managed to fetch his head after it was chopped off.

The fey piss him off on principle.

Adrianna pops up beside him, striding quickly, matching his longer gait. He slows for her.

Slash understands she is a crippling weakness in his otherwise-iron-clad defenses.

He is also desperately in love with her.

"Hey," she says softly.

Slash says hello back, keeping his face in profile, relieved she's on the good side of his face. Adrianna doesn't seem to notice that Slash is purposefully hiding his face.

"What do you think about all this?" she asks.

Slash takes a painful, dry swallow. Her nearness is undoing his thoughts.

Slash remains vigilant, scanning the surrounding area for threats.

"Slash," Adrianna says, reminding him that she asked a question.

He forgets his looks for a few seconds and braves a glance at her, his nostrils flaring subtly.

Her hair is everywhere, messy from the battle and their pace. Her hazel eyes are very wide and bright. Slash wants to count the freckles that are so like captured gold flakes in pale skin running over the bridge of her nose.

"Slash," Adrianna says again.

Slash realizes he stopped walking, and he stares at her.

"I made my piece known during our brief talk," he replies, referring to the group decision to bring Tharell.

"Pfft," Adrianna sounds off, beginning to walk again, and a breath of relief eases out of his tight chest. "You didn't make your piece known. You insulted the vamp and the fey."

Slash shrugs. *The fey? And what of them?* They were corrupt, wanting to siphon off the Singers' numbers and literally bring hell to earth with what Tharell did using his demonic connection. No. Slash is *not* inclined toward forgiveness or camaraderie.

He smiles, and the scar tissue on his face tightens.

Adrianna, seeing only the good part of his profile, smiles in return. "True. However, I don't care. The fey are a part of anything that involves what they can get.

Slash allows a snort, and it comes out like a snuffle. "And the Were aren't?"

He looks over his shoulder at the Were who survived the massacre and he is not surprised to see Zeke give a microscopic chin lift when Slash's scrutiny rolls over him.

"We are. But we're cleaner about it."

A dark-blonde eyebrow lifts. "That makes it better, hmm?"

No, but it is easier. Slash remains silent under what he perceives as her condemnation.

Adrianna sighs, grabs his hand, and slings his entire arm over her shoulders.

Slash's heart races, and his palms tingle at the unexpected contact.

Her nostrils flare. "Do I scent fear on you, Slash?" Her question is serious, her voice coy.

His feelings are a dangerous game.

No use lying. "Yes."

Slash keeps walking, his arm around the female Alpha Were he would mate if allowed, if he were not marred.

"Of me?" she whispers.

He nods.

He guides them deeper into the edge of the forest. The caravan of supernaturals continue to walk toward where members of Region Two are waiting to drive them back to One, to the false perception of safety.

Slash relaxes in the shadows, his ugly mug hidden from Adrianna.

He turns to face her fully, his large hands cradling her face. "I cannot have you, Adrianna. You must wait for someone from your den who is worthy of you."

Slash's self-loathing has never been deeper, wider, or more intense. He has to break it off with Adrianna and take away the hope of their being together. Slash can't handle her eventual rejection when another Were decides he wants her. And that Were will be whole and perfect, without the scars of war on his mind—or his face.

"Oh Slash," Adrianna says softly, cupping her smaller hand over his and he scents things that confuse him.

Truth.

Desire.

"I have found a male worthy of me. And there is no other," she says in the ancient language, and it fingers a chord like a guitar string inside Slash, as though a melody has begun playing just for him.

The Singers claim their blood sings to the vampire and Were alike.

Slash believes certain blood ties are just as strong between the right pair—the perfect mating pair.

"Adrianna, I'm broken. Can't you see it?" His eyes implore her to see what is so obvious, to heed reason.

She shakes her head, sending her ratty hair, stained and dirty from fighting at his side, sliding over shoulders.

Slash smiles.

My brave girl.

"You're not gonna do this, Slash."

He frowns. "Do what?"

"Hide—sacrifice."

Her hand leaves his and she slides her arms around his neck as her fingers grip his nape.

"No," Slash says in a panic, beginning to pull away, his hands dropping from her face.

"Yes," she says, "a million times, yes."

Then the softest skin he has ever felt brushes his lips, feathering over the scar tissue like heated silk. The barest breath of moisture flicks at the seam of his mouth, and his lips part against his volition.

Slash forgets the promises made to himself.

He forgets he is in the middle of a dangerous return to Region One and that others besides him are in danger.

And most importantly, Slash forgets how fractured he is. In Adrianna's arms, he is whole.

She moves to her tiptoes, gripping his neck more tightly and hanging off him.

With a groan of consent, Slash bends down and lifts Adrianna off her feet. She's above him now, her legs around his waist, her fingers grasping the fuzz of hair that covers his head. Her thumb lands on one of the horrible scars on his skull, and he can't pull away. He doesn't want to.

She kisses him deeply, her tongue diving inside his mouth, and he moans, hardening helplessly against her. She laughs softly against his mouth.

"I knew you liked me."

And that's where it ends for Slash.

He loosens her hold on him, gently letting her slide down the front of him, every hard inch in stark relief. He is embarrassed by his obvious arousal, but there's nothing he can do. He is a male Were, and she is the female he desires.

The only one.

He captures her wrists behind her back as his forehead touches hers. "That's the thing I'm trying to explain."

She speaks to his chest. "What? What is it Slash. You are the Were for me. You've always been."

"I don't like you," Slash says.

Their eyes meet.

"What are you saying?" Her gaze looks uncertain now, and shadows of doubt linger in the lightest part of her eyes.

"I don't like you—I love you," Slash says so quietly, his words are barely more than mouthed syllables.

Humiliated, he turns his back on Adrianna. However, now that she knows he's serious over her, she'll back off. He's too much work. Slash understands this.

He feels a tap on his shoulder, and he stubbornly stays facing the woods, his arms folded. He stares, memorizing every furrow of bark, every pine cone, and each needle.

Then Adrianna is standing before him.

"Hey!" she shoves him in the chest, and he takes a step back, frowning. "You"—she pushes—"don't get to play father confessor then give me the cold shoulder." She slaps his chest again, and he grabs her arms.

She bares her teeth, and his wolf responds, growling.

Slash tightens his hold, taking deep breaths to steady his animal. The urge to dominate her and take her as his wolf wants to causes him to throb painfully.

He looks away, but he can't bring himself to let go of her. He doesn't know if he'll ever be able to. *Dammit, I'm trying to do the right thing. The honorable thing. Why can't she see it?*

He asks her fiercely, "Then what would you have of me?" He looks down at the beautiful mouth he just kissed and falls off the precipice of reason. "Since you already have my heart."

She runs a finger down the worst of the scarring of his face and he flinches. "Look at me, Slash."

He barely lifts his chin, his nostrils flaring at her heady scent. He needs to get the hell out of here, and fast. Or his wolf will act for him. It's so close to the surface of his skin he can see the microscopic movement of his flesh rippling.

Her hazel eyes drill into his. And his wolf likes the dominant display of the female—his female.

"I love you, too, you big damn dope." She takes her finger away and punches him in the arm. "I'm not going anywhere, and I don't give two shits and an eff if you have scars. Or if you've killed a legion of Were in battle. Or that you're not in my pack."

Slash's chest is so tight, he can't draw a single breath. His emotions drown him, clogging his airways.

Adrianna puts her hand on his chest then grips his shirt in her small fist. "*Hear* me, Slash."

His eyes pull to hers.

"Lawrence can stick it up his ass. I want *you*."

Slash covers her hands with his own, and the steel bands around his chest loosen. She renounced her pack-master so easily.

"Female, you—you ease me." And she does, so much. If only Slash didn't feel guilty for this moment of stolen happiness.

Adrianna's grin is fierce, and certain. "I know."

He smiles back, but it feels a little sad around the edges. "For how long will you be with me? I am not casual in my affections." It's such an understatement, it's utterly ludicrous to voice.

"Duh. Slash, I *get* this. You're old-school. I couldn't like another wolf if he bit me on the ass." She laughs.

Slash growls at the thought of any Were touching her, especially *there*.

"You goofball," she sinks against him, laying her face against his muscular chest.

He holds one of her hands between their bodies and wraps his free hand around her back, pressing her tightly against him.

"Don't you know? I've always been yours."

He lays the unscarred side of his face against the top of her head.

Praile

*P*raile's long ebony tail is held high. It twitches, making a slight whistling sound as it whips to and fro.

That usually happens when Praile's irritated. He's highly irritated now.

Praile grasps Anthony Daniel Laurent by the hair. He shakes Anthony's head slightly. The eyes have already glazed over with the whitish icy-gray shroud of death. With a disgusted snort, Praile chucks the severed head onto the pile of bodies.

He sees Tony's prick like a blackened flesh noodle and holds in a laugh.

Not bad. Judging by the wound, it was torn off his body by teeth. Praile snickers, not bothering to contain his glee. He taps a taloned finger on his chin, considering. *He might not have done as well.*

Praile is a systematic high demon who is not wont to being dramatic. But jerking Tony's penis off with his teeth would have come with a certain amount of satisfaction, though the action was a tad intimate for his taste, which ran to the female persuasion.

As humans have assumed for millennia, there is no pleasure to be had in Hades. But there is much to be had on this plane. Praile's sharp eyesight takes in the nuances of death all around him.

One important instrument of advancement and justice is missing—the death saber. It brings death to nearly all supernaturals. Praile scans the bodies—they're all demonic.

The Singers must have buried their own.

He whistles in the fifty-HZ range of ultrasonic frequencies that only canines can hear, and three demons swivel their heads in Praile's direction. He jerks his jaw, gesturing for them to join him.

They move. They're obedient That is good, because the consequence for disobedience is swift and unyielding—very much like hell.

Lazarus comes first. His unflattering pale-red skin and unadorned tail notwithstanding, he is the very best high demon Praile has ever known. He will kill anything, and he is built perfectly for the strenuous physical demands of their kind: to torture anything that breathes.

And he is so exacting about it all. His name always makes Praile take hidden jest—it's an apt nickname. Lazarus can bring most back from true death. *Oh, the irony!*

Praile speculates Lazarus has a little Singer blood. That Healer part of him is handy during torture in the hot place.

Praile hides his giddy expression with difficulty, loving his own humor. After all, Praile is his own biggest fan.

His brow furrows. The Master will not find the minions' failure to kill all the Singers humorous or appreciate their inability to capture the two most important females in a thousand years.

Yet, Praile finds it all so droll.

He longs for a true challenge and to have more freedom on this plane to torture, maim, and antagonize. *After all, what fun is being a demon if one cannot spread darkness and cruelty?*

Praile folds his muscular arms. "Speak," he barks at Lazarus. He smirks at his second-in-command, silently daring him to address his abhorrent interaction.

But Lazarus is too clever to take the bait, which causes Praile a perverse joy. *One must take small joys whenever they are presented.*

Praile sulks quietly at Lazarus's utter lack of reaction. Lazarus is self-contained in a way that is rare of the aggressive demonic, and it pains Praile.

"Some of our soldiers have escaped. The others have met true death."

Praile casts a glance at the low demons who accompany him and Lazarus. He dismisses them when they lower their eyes in subservient deference.

"What of the Angelic Blood?"

Lazarus heaves an exhale of disgust. "She is not here."

"Really?" Praile asks sarcastically, stepping into his second's space. *Fool.*

Lazarus doesn't flinch.

So brave, Lazarus. "I know *that,*" Praile spits.

I so loathe relying on others, however necessary.

"I scent the High One's blood."

Praile whips his head back in Lazarus's direction, flaring his nostrils. He tastes the truth of Lazarus's words on his tongue. "Really?" he says without the sarcasm he'd employed earlier.

"Yes."

Praile runs his eyes over Lazarus. *What a shame he doesn't possess the fine deep-scarlet skin that his kind finds so beautiful.* It's also unfortunate that Lazarus cannot have the tail that ends with an appendage of weaponry.

His eyes narrow at Lazarus. It might be just as well that the other demonic is lacking, for Praile would be even more jealous of Lazarus than he already is. Praile hates his own perceived lack of gifts.

Lazarus's keen sense of smell rivals that of the Were. It is so acute, he can scent emotions, where Praile can scent only a lie. Lazarus can take every drop of life out of anything that draws breath and give it back at will. He has also animated the dead for his bidding.

Useful attributes in a demonic.

That bit was something to see. Commanding the dead, as a demonic, is a rare gift. But Lazarus is ugly. Certainly, with his sculpted face, square jaw, and tall muscled body, he might appeal to some demon females as a pity fuck.

Praile is picky about his dalliances, though. He cocks his head. Actually, he's discerning about everything. He shrugs.

"Is she wounded?"

Lazarus nods, serious and, as usual, humorless.

Praile licks his lips. "Do tell."

Lazarus makes loose fists. "She has a piece of us inside her."

Praile chortles. "Excellent."

"The High One is still mortal?" Praile's gaze searches Lazarus's.

Lazarus smiles, showing bright, ugly white teeth. "Absolutely."

Praile lets out a sigh of relief. *All is not lost.*

"Idiots, they should have wedded her. Were, vampire, and Singer. And the Angelic Blood would be untouchable. Though it would be a great source of amusement to kill all who served her," Praile muses.

Lazarus does a poor job of containing his irritation.

"Let us fetch the death saber. We can't have that in the wrong hands, though I am most pleased Anthony managed to pierce the Angelic Blood before his cock and balls were chewed off his worthless body."

The low demons mewl from their safe position several feet away from Praile.

His grin widens, showing off his ebony teeth to perfection.

"You two"—he swings a black talon-tipped finger toward two of his minions—"clean up the mess of your kind and go to hell."

A giggle bubbles in Praile's throat, and he barely suppresses it. He gives Lazarus a sidelong glance to ascertain if his second noticed his slippage.

Lazarus meets his eyes but finally ends the staring contest.

It is well-known that high demons have a propensity to slide into madness after middle age. At over seven hundred years old, Praile is no exception. Yet he must finish the Master's most important work.

The High One shall be slain.

The abomination growing inside the belly of the mixed-blood royal Singer shall be sacrificed in Hades, as prophesied.

A child destined to have the blood of all cannot be allowed to survive—or save the Angelic Blood through the gift of immortality.

The last task of the Master is a tall order.

Praile is just the demon to fill it.

Julia

A mansion even more grand than Region One's rises on a perfectly shaped knoll like a jewel that's lost its luster. Its paint is peeling, and the once-grand dame stands in testimony as a shell of her former self. It deepens Julia's depression. If she can make it through the next day, she'll be so thankful.

Jason and the other Were get practical and melt back into full human form, Cyn and Adi stay in quarter-change form, though. Julia would stay that way all the time if she were a female Were.

She admires Cyn's and Adi's versatility in a world that is harsh on the subsect of humanity that dwindles under their noses.

All these groups were co-existing with her for her entire life, and she'd never known.

Slash and Adi walk together toward the front entrance, where the large oak door stands open.

Slash gives a look at the Were, and the Reds, including the new Alaskan Red, Zeke, jogging to his position.

"What is it?" Julia whispers, suddenly feeling the weight of silence that surrounds them. This, where Jacqueline once reigned, is the first region headquarters Julia has ever been to, other than her own.

She swallows the lump of sadness suddenly lodged in her throat. The one that Marcus put there, the same one she gets thinking of Scott, the sole survivor of Tony's massacre.

In truth, Scott survived only if Tom Harriet and his goons didn't kill both him and Lucius. She breathes through the painful thought of Scott being expunged from this earth. Julia can't imagine the world without him in it. Julia doesn't know what that sentiment means for her—or for Jason.

"It's all about the recon, babe," Jason says, laying a kiss on her forehead.

She leans against him, her body fitting perfectly against his.

A whisper of an exhale slides out of her tight body. "Right," she says, and even to her own ears, she sounds unconvinced.

Jason cups the back of her head with his hand. "I don't blame ya—it's been a thing. This whole entire last week has been nothing but one calamity after a-fucking-nother."

I agree. Though Julia doesn't bother saying it out loud. There's really no need.

Julia's tension remains, though she knows she's safe in Jason's arms while the Were file through the house.

Her eyes meet Jacqueline's. Julia stalls when she sees the slight swell to Jacqueline's belly.

"Hang on," Julia says, walking toward her.

Jacqueline turns to her.

Domi's silver eyes glitter at Julia, and she decides she won't be unnerved by it. Barely.

"Hey," Julia says a little breathlessly, her hand straying to where her stomach wound was a day ago.

"Hello," Jacqueline replies in her smooth voice. She glances at Julia's palm on her stomach. "How does your wound fare?"

"It's okay, I guess."

Jacqueline frowns. "That's more evasion than reply."

Julia gives her a crooked smile. "Can't pull much over on you."

"No." Jacqueline gives a minute shake of her head.

"It feels weird to be your friend now," Julia blurts then almost covers her mouth.

Jacqueline nods. "I know exactly what you mean."

Domi moves behind her, lifting her dark hair away from her neck so he can lay his palm at her nape, and though Julia doesn't think she's aware, Jacqueline tips her jaw into the small embrace. Domi's eyes soften at the gesture.

Oh, my word, there's some stuff going on there.

Stay on task, Julia. "I noticed you're looking all pregnant."

Their eyes catch and hold. Jacqueline glances away first. "Yes," she says in a low voice, "Domi postulates there's an accelerated pace of gestation."

"Ah. Okay," Julia replies slowly, looking form one to the other. "Is this normal? I mean, for a fey baby?"

Domi lifts his chin. His navy hair, like midnight liquid, gleams as it slides over his shoulders. Not a hair is out of place. They've battled and haven't showered or eaten. Everyone is beat, yet Domi looks as fresh as a daisy—except for that healing scar at his throat.

Julia tears her eyes away from the scrutiny of his neck and he smiles at her blatant curiosity. She feels her cheeks heat. *Nice, Julia.*

She glances at the Were moving in and out of the house then looks back at Domi and Jacqueline.

"No," Domi says in a voice so melodic, it doesn't sound natural but like spoken music. "We think the babe is special."

"Of course it is," Julia says, giving Jacqueline a tentative smile.

"What Domi means is that the genetics of the baby are dictating some unusual beginnings."

Julia stares at Jacqueline. "You mean, like some kind of one-of-a-kind kid?"

Jacqueline smiles so suddenly and naturally, it startles Julia. Sadly, the woman smiles so infrequently that the expression sits oddly on her face. "I forget your way with words. But yes, we believe the baby will be...very unusual."

"He will be fey, Were, vampire, Singer, and angelic," Domi says with a casual lift of his shoulder.

"Oh, well, no big deal then," Julia says with a small laugh. "Like Heinz 57, guys."

They give identical puzzled expressions, and Julia laughs again. "You guys. Okay, are we sure all that mingling of cool genes is the reason for Jacqueline to have a speed pregnancy?"

"It is conjecture," Domi admits.

Jacqueline rubs her cheek against his fingers, and his shoulders relax. "It sounds like the right fit, as you would say," Jacqueline says.

Their eyes meet again. It *is* what Julia would have said. Jacqueline's intuition is uncanny.

"Are you sad about going back to faerie?"

Jacqueline's eyes round, and she grips Domi's hand. His eyes harden, his irises unpolished diamonds.

Whoa.

"No. I can be who I was meant to be in the mound, near the sithen. Without it, I am the Jacqueline of old."

Don't want that.

"Hey, Jules," Jason says from behind her, his eyes wary on Jacqueline, and for good reason.

"All's clear. They're rounding up the rigs now."

Julia turns to say goodbye for the moment to Jacqueline, but her dark eyes stay locked on the old headquarters where she formerly reigned. Silent tears are streaming down her face.

Domi turns Jacqueline to face him, lightly gripping her shoulders. He passes one hand over her face, and when it comes away, he cups his palm beneath her jaw.

Her tears fall in perfect teardrop formation, tinkling together inside his palm in hardened clear gems.

"What? What did you do?" Jason asks. The awe in his voice matches Julia's feelings.

"Tears are precious in faerie. We do not waste emotion. Some can be collected."

Jacqueline gives him a tremulous smile, rolling her bottom lip between her teeth to stop the shaking.

"That's the coolest thing I've ever seen," Julia says under her breath as Jason takes her hand.

Domi gives a small shrug. "It's a parlor trick."

"No," Julia say, meeting his eyes, "You took her sadness and made it your own."

Domi says nothing, assenting to the truth of the words through lack of reply.

He pockets the jewels of Jacqueline's sadness, and she places her hand over where they lay.

The car ride is terrible. The black, unmarked SUVs are luxurious, built to last, and anonymous. They riot through the night like oil-slicked bullets.

But Julia knows what awaits them at the Region One headquarters—emptiness.

The voices of the children will be absent. Scott and Lucius are unaccounted for. The beautiful lake that is filled with swans, is now surrounded by a mass grave.

Her only consolation is that the murdering jerk-off is dead. *But what's happened to the Greenes? And what about Reagan? Delilah?*

Julia can't sleep on the way home. Tumultuous thoughts spin inside her brain on an endless cycle. Wedged between Adi and Jason, she leans her head against Jason's shoulder. The men *have the door*, as they so succinctly put it. It was super-funny to Julia when they said the women would be in the middle and they should ride on the outside, in case of disaster.

Uh-huh. Adi said it best: "Me, Tarzan. You, Jane."

Slash scowled. Then had brightened when Adi scolded him.

Men.

They broke every speed limit and stopped for gas only once. The Were moved around outside, and Tharell lay gagged and bound in the back of one of the SUVs.

Julia swore she could feel his eyes on her through all that disastrous metal that he hated so much.

Domi threw up. Even with Jacqueline and his unborn child offering a buffer of sorts, the metal of the car was too much for him.

They finally arrive and everyone pours out of the vehicles after they park in the gigantic circular drive in front of the Victorian.

Warm lights don't illuminate the windows.

The house stands like four corners of stark in the middle of grief. A symbol of what was.

Julia stays in the car. She looks at the training barn, then away. She remembers when Michael made the pile of manure to contain Scott and a smile hovers on her lips without becoming.

Scott.

Julia shivers at the thought of her soul-meld. Guilt and indecision shake her to the core. Getting out of the rig is accepting that she's back, in charge of a new beginning with a future that's completely unknown.

She doesn't know if it's the beginning she wants.

Jason comes back to the SUV and leans against the open door. He braces his biceps against the door frame and leans in. "What are you doing here, looking all sad and shit? We're here. Let's clean up, eat some grub."

Jason reaches forward, cups her chin, then slides his fingertips from her temple to her jaw. She catches his hand as it retreats.

"Come on, Jules," Jason says, pulling her out of the vehicle.

She follows, his hand warm in hers.

Julia ignores the ache that plagues her belly.

7

Tessa

" *H*oly mother of the moon, that was a damn mess back there," Tessa says, throwing her eyes to Tahlia then back at the road.

Tahlia's as quiet as the tomb.

"Hey listen, honey—I'm just running blind here. You gotta give me something to go on." Tessa heaves a sigh, flipping her wayward braid out of the way. "I mean, who do you belong to?"

Tahlia's fingers worry at her borrowed shirt that's at least two sizes too big. She's a wisp of a girl. Dark skin and hair frame eyes so deep a blue, they're almost violet. The shock of her curly hair misses frizzy by a millimeter, but her exotic blend is obvious. She's unique for a Were. There are Were of every race, but it's very rare for a mix. And a mix as lovely as this girl—Wereshifter—is unheard of.

"Tell me *something*," Tessa pleads.

Tahlia seems to decide something, though her face is like carved stone. "I am of the Lanarre."

Lycan royalty. Good gravy. "What?" Tessa shrieks, gripping the wheel to maintain control and not run the car off the road.

Tahlia winces. "That is why I said nothing."

Tessa narrows her eyes on Tahlia. "I understand some of the protocols. You're a whelp."

Her chin lifts in the first defiance Tessa's seen out of the girl. "I am of age."

Tessa flicks her eyes over Tahlia once, shifts her eyes to the road, then comes back to her. "No way."

A light blush spreads across the girl's cheeks.

"You would be held by human guardians while traveling away from the pack." The Lanarre often bred humans to act as their guardians from one generation to the next.

Tahlia inhales a shuddering breath that sounds both hollow and grief stricken.

"What?" Tessa breathes, automatically lifting her foot off the accelerator.

"They were murdered."

Something doesn't make sense. And we're going to flesh it right out.

"A rogue Were…" Tahlia's wide eyes move to Tessa in apparent apology.

Tessa dismisses her trepidation curtly. "It's okay. I know what I am."

She sighs in relief then continues, "He came and slaughtered everyone in the rented domicile where we lodged."

Hotel.

"You speak strangely," Tessa interjects.

"I speak as I am meant to."

Okay. Wrong tactic.

"Go on," Tessa encourages, rolling her hand in a circle.

"My human guardians were allowing me to watch the television." Her eyes spark. "It is strictly forbidden," she admits in hushed tones.

Unreal. Talk about living in a bubble. But Tessa remains rapt, saying nothing.

"The guardians are just extraordinary humans. They do not share our senses."

Tessa nods. *Of course not.*

"We had the television turned up quite loud for my guardians benefit." That made sense as what humans thought was the correct volume would sting a Were's sensitive hearing.

"I—" Tahlia wrings her hands, which bleed to white under the pressure.

Guilt, Tessa realizes.

"Don't," Tessa interrupts, putting her hand over the girl's. "There was nothing to be done, nothing you could have done."

She bites her lip, and fat tears fall straight from her eyes to her clenched hands.

"I needed to use the restroom and excused myself to—ah!" She tears her hands from underneath Tessa's and covers her face. "I listened and did nothing!" she yells.

Tessa grits her teeth against Tahlia's shame. She empathizes. Tessa pulls over onto the soft shoulder, letting the old car idle.

She takes Tahlia's hands into her own. "Listen up, Tahlia. There's no way you could have done anything but get dead."

Tahlia nods reluctantly. "I understand." She bites her lip. "But it does not make it any easier to suffer the truth. They are still gone from this earth, Tessa."

"You saved me, and I didn't matter."

"Everyone matters," Tahlia answers softly.

They share a look and a sudden laugh.

"You know how to make short work of Weres," Tessa says.

A tentative smile graces her full lips. "They were not of good intent. And my animal does what I cannot."

"No shit?" Tessa says, and the girl's eyes bug. She gives Tahlia a speculative look.

"You know, you're kind of sheltered."

Tahlia shakes her head. "Not really. My duty is set. It has been ordained since my infancy."

Tessa wracks her brain for memories of the fabled Lanarre, but all she comes up with is that they are the elite of the Were, all Alphas. Anyone born a Lanarre is automatically an Alpha.

"What duty?" Tessa asks.

"My duty to the Lanarre," she replies slowly, as if Tessa is a dim-witted child.

Tessa relaxes in the seat, giving Tahlia steady eyes. An idea, an ugly one, forms in the back of her mind.

"What were you doing out of the safety of the Lanarre, traveling with your human guards?"

"I was traveling to meet my chosen."

Oh, my moon.

"What chosen?"

Tahlia tries to put a blanket over her disgust of Tessa's lack of knowledge. "Are the ways of the Lycan so diluted that the packs no longer know how we came to be? Our history."

Tessa shrugs. "I guess not." She was usually too busy running from Tramack to concern herself with Lycan history.

Tahlia makes a noise in the back of her throat. "My chosen is the male who will be my mate."

Tessa gulps back disgust. "You're telling me this is some kind of arranged marriage?"

Tahlia lifts a shoulder and eyebrow simultaneously. "Were do not marry, as you know."

"Right," Tessa acknowledges, "but to mate a male Were—"

"Lanarre," Tahlia corrects.

"Uh-huh. Sight unseen? Do you have a choice?"

The girl's delicate brows pull together. "Why do I need one? He is my chosen."

Repeating it over and over again doesn't make it a great plan in Tessa's view. "What if he's a sadistic pig?" Tessa asks.

A laugh erupts from Tahlia's throat. "Are you having me on? You are very negative, Tessa."

Yes, yes I am. It kept her butt safe for more years than she could count. *And this arranged mating thing? It stinks to high heaven.*

"I have a question of you," Tahlia says.

Tessa hikes her eyebrows. "Shoot."

The girl gives a slight frown. "May I smell you?"

Tessa's chin juts back. "I guess—but weird."

"Humor me."

She sounds so old for a whelp.

Tahlia leans close, rising to her knees as she moves in, then takes a whiff of Tess from neck to crotch.

A human would blanch at such a gesture.

If asked, it's not an exceptional thing among Were.

But of all the things the girl could ask about, she chose scenting.

Tahlia sits back against her heels.

"You smell of him."

Huh? "Who?" Tessa searches her face in the growing shadows. She sees everything. The time of day or night doesn't matter.

Gooseflesh rises at the expectation of the revelation.

"The one who murdered my guardians."

Fuck. Her heart sinks.

Tessa knew she should have drowned that crazy Were in the ditch.

She leans away from Tahlia, collapsing against the back of the driver's seat.

Now who's the guilty one? If she had followed her instincts, Tahlia's guardians would be alive. And according to her gruesome testimony, a lot of other innocents would be, too.

Tessa closes her eyes.

"Tell me why the murderer of my human guardians scent is all over you."

"I should have killed his ass when I had the chance."

"Tell me," Tahlia commands intensely.

The women sit in the silent car when the last word from Tessa echoes within.

"That is an awful tale."

"Not as bad as me letting that screwed up male live."

Tahlia draws a painful sounding inhale. "You could not have known."

Tessa shoots a sharp look at Tahlia. "He almost killed you."

A slight smile lifts the corners of her mouth. "There would have been a wrath unlike any the Lycans would have known at my death."

Do I hear a smug note to that comment? Tessa searches Tahlia's face. No, she stated it like fact.

Maybe it is.

"I am the princess of my people."

High Alpha female.

"Oh, shit," Tessa breathes in reply.

Tahlia nods. "Yes." Then, she says, "You have very colorful language."

"Yup." Tessa turns to her, ignoring the relevance of that last. "Do you want to mate with this guy?"

"Drek?"

Tessa nods. "Is he the…prince of something."

Tahlia's lips curl. "High Alpha male."

Knew it. "Yes, him."

Her eyes slide away from Tessa. "Of course."

Hell no she doesn't.

"Is he an okay guy, like…"

"I do not know if he is a 'sadistic pig.'" She gives a little grin, ducking her head, and Tessa laughs. The girl has a great sense of humor buried underneath all the layers of propriety.

"Okay, so can we just do whatever? Stick together? Or do you have parents or what?"

Her face smooths.

Tessa knows masked sadness when she sees it.

"I do not know my parents. Only my guardians. One to guard and one to take care of me and teach me the ways of the Lanarre."

That's awful.

"Okay," Tessa slaps her thighs, knowing the girl essentially just lost the only caregivers she ever knew. "So let's take the long way."

"The which?"

Tessa grins, throwing the car into gear. "Let's show up when we feel like it."

Tahlia bites her lip and Tessa realizes that's her nervous tell.

"They will search for me."

Tessa snorts. "Have at it, guys." She turns and relaxes against the seat. Tessa hears the seatbelt click.

"I think I like you, Tessa."

"I like you, too, Tahlia. I always think people that save my life are the best." Tessa winks at Tahlia, and a shy smile ghosts her lips.

Neither one of them have a friend in the world.

But it looks like they have each other.

Things could be worse.

Praile

The barbed end of the lash checks the top layer of his skin and peels it away like sliced cheese.

Praile gnashes his black teeth together as a layer of smoldering mist hovers above his flesh.

Praile always smolders when his emotions run high.

The lash whistles a high note at the return. It sings as it returns to meet his flesh.

Praile bellows as the thirteenth lash strikes deep, ringing its poison-tipped metal on a vertebrae in his fileted back.

"Halt," a low voice says from behind Praile. His head bows to his chest. Rivulets of sweat burn a pathway through his scalp and pour down to fill the wounds the barbed lashes have made on the entire length of his spine.

Praile dare not turn. The next lash might paralyze him. Yes, he could heal it, but the vulnerability of not feeling or being able to move would be his undoing as his skills of self-healing were greatly limited. Healing is not one of his gifts.

"I believe Praile has learned a valuable lesson this day," the Master comments.

He has learned nothing except if something were to go ill, Praile will suffer. However, The Master has taught Praile well, and he emulates the Master.

"Release him from his bindings."

Two of the low demons appear at either side of Praile and unshackle him. One dares to meet his eyes.

The gaze of the low contains a measured triumph. He is pleased by Praile's punishment.

Praile grins, marking him for later, and he bows his head, scuttling away.

Run faster, minion.

The Master slithers to Praile, the swish of his robes is all that Praile hears.

Praile feels real fear, which is rare. His gaze drops, concentrating on the hem of the Master's robe. The Master's feet are grotesquely disproportionate. Long cracked black toenails that are so long, they nearly curl.

The Master always smolders.

A black mist rises from the flesh of his feet. His toes wiggle and Praile flinches.

The Master chuckles a dark note of contentment into the hot cavern where torture, death, and discipline are meted.

"You are a good slave to the cause, Praile. However, when you called the Were to destroy our enemies on earth, the one who was most important to be slain runs about unharmed. And the Blood Babe lives inside the womb of a crafty Singer. One who is a female after my own heart."

Praile hears a dull thump as the Master's meaty fist thumps his own chest.

The lump in Praile's throat shifts, stifling his breathing.

"I am entrusting you to find this Singer that is with child. *The* child."

A talon touches the fleshy part of Praile's chin, and he winces, though it does not hurt.

"Bring her to me." The Master's rancid breath bathes Praile's face.

Praile turns away, for even he cannot bear it.

The Master laughs at his discomfiture. "Kill the Angelic Blood, the High One. Do not hesitate. Do not tarry. Bring me the whites of the Angelic's eyes."

"Yes, Master," Praile whispers.

"I will make your death last for an eon if you fail me in this."

Praile knows. He nods.

The Master's hands thread through his hair, slowly squeezing like a vise. "Are we clear, Praile?"

His meaning is utterly clear as the Master's fingerprints begin to burn into Praile's scalp.

"Yes."

His grips tightens to the point of screeching pain, then he abruptly releases Praile's head.

Praile bites back his relief and begins to control his breathing, concentrating only on that.

"Lazarus will heal your wounds—yet not perfectly. You should feel the pain as a reminder of what yet needs accomplishing."

Praile lays his palms against the heated stone in front of him, trying not to notice the lost talons embedded in the wall from failed escapes by the masses tortured before him. The black blood has faded over time to a washed-out charcoal. It fills the grooves and divots of the nearly black rock.

Praile groans as he straightens, keeping his eyes away from the Master. To look upon him is sure insanity. No one has ever cast their eyes upon the Master and lived to tell of it.

Their screams were silenced.

Praile shudders as a talon caresses the most grievous wound at his back.

"I will see to it." Praile's agony drips from each word.

The talon sinks deep, and Praile bites the inside of his cheek until the rich taste of copper fills his mouth as he suffers through the inspection of the fresh wound on his back.

"Good." The talon lifts, and Praile nearly weeps in relief.

Praile's shoulders slump as the Master exits the chamber. He stays in the same tense position until Lazarus appears at his side.

Praile's hate for Lazarus burns brightly. But Lazarus does his job.

"This will be more painful before it heals, Praile."

"Yes, *yes*. Get on with it."

Fingers dig inside the wounds, and Praile squeals like a pig brought to slaughter. The pain is so acute, he forgets to breathe—or think. He arches to escape the probing fingertips, but nothing will relieve him.

"Hold him up," Lazarus murmurs.

Low demons, whom Praile does not know, hoist him by the armpits as the searing healing begins.

"Stop," he moans.

"No," Lazarus replies.

Praile is sure he hears a smile in that one-word reply.

He opens his mouth to convey the pain Lazarus will incur for his joy at his master's pain.

But the pain is too great. It rips at his brain, and all falls to blackness.

The demonic can camouflage their bodies. If the demonic did not have this ability, humans could easily call them out. Though Praile's skin is the coveted deepest red of his kind, it is well outside of human norms. And when he is rife with emotion, he smolders and small stubby horns sprout above his head. Though they are a sign of beauty for the demonic, they are an instant warning to humans that he is *other*.

Lazarus does not have horns, beautiful dark skin, or a tail weapon. He can be camouflaged easily and fit in nicely among humankind. Lazarus, with his horrible white teeth, hornless head, and lackluster tail, has less to hide.

He is the perfect lackey.

Praile will need to remain calm. High demons have a more difficult time hiding what they are.

Three days have passed since the Master's punishment. Lazarus healed Praile three quarters to right, and no more, according to specific instruction.

Praile cannot mask his stiffness. Though the deepest wound is sealed halfway, it seeps through the ridiculous human costume he is forced to wear. The cotton button-down shirt is sticking to the wet wounds of his back, and it pulls as he takes breaths.

Praile holds up his palm, and Lazarus slows, putting large hands on his denim-clad hips.

"Wait."

Lazarus cocks a light red eyebrow. "If you need rest…"

Praile rolls his eyes. "Of course I need rest!" he bellows into the still night air. "It is not about *rest*, Lazarus. Our Master requires this task completed in a timely way." Praile pants, trying to straighten. Unable to manage it, he hunches once more.

"Flag down a human vehicle so that we might make haste to where the Angelic resides."

Lazarus frowns. "It is a risk I advise you not to take."

Praile straightens, hissing as the material of the shirt sticks to his tender back. "Duly noted. Now flag. Down. A. Human."

"What if the human possesses the devices of sanctity?"

Drat.

"Crosses and the like?" Lazarus prompts as though Praile needs a reminder.

Praile's brows drop like bricks above his eyes, and a lazy smolder begins above the bare skin at the back of his hands. "It is unlikely, with so many humans in thrall with evil, that we will come across the random practitioner."

"There is the matter of an Angelic among humanity."

Praile staggers toward Lazarus, looking up at the taller male, hating his stature. "You let me divine which human is a threat to us."

"My discernment—"

"Your discernment is a tool in my arsenal, Lazarus—do not forget that."

Lazarus allows a rare show of emotion, his lips curling as he bares his teeth. "You do not let me," he says.

Lazarus makes his way from the forest where the portal of Hades empties to the highway, and which the human masses use to scurry from one ant hill to the next.

Praile narrows his gaze at Lazarus's broad back.

I will be watching you. Praile follows, making his slow and painful ascent from the gulley toward the highway.

Slash

$\mathcal{S}$ lash remains on edge. Though the fey disposed of the gruesome remains of the decimated Singer population, the taste of death lingers over Region One like a stench that will never be cleansed.

Zeke of the rogue Alaskan Were stands at Slash's side. "So many dead can't be so easily covered up." His nose wrinkles.

Slash grunts his assent and paces away. "What are our numbers?" He turns back, and Zeke shrugs.

"Bad."

That's what Slash was afraid of. The demonic killed nearly half of the Region Two Singers, leaving roughly fifty behind. And half of those are children. As is typical, Slash wants hard numbers for fighters. Many are unaccounted for.

What of Lawrence and Manny?

"Do we have a superb tracker? Can we know for certain who is dead?"

Zeke shakes his head. His exotic looks are unusual for the lower forty-eight, though Native Americans were plentiful where Zeke's pack ran in the north. "Our numbers are down by half, too. Our best tracker—gone."

Slash remembers something. "Jacqueline, the Singer from Two, she's a Tracker."

Zeke nods slowly, but his brows drop low over his eyes. "Do we want to use her? She is with child and has—what should we say?—bad blood." Zeke laughs at the inside joke.

Slash can't bring himself to.

Zeke studies him for a moment. "You're a serious wolf."

Slash nods. "Serious times are afoot, Red."

Zeke stares at him for a second more. Instead of answering, he melds into his wolfen form.

Slash's laugh sounds like a bark, as he's changed, as well. Athletic pants expand to fit his increased girth and height, though he doesn't wear a shirt. "Perimeter sweep?"

Zeke nods, and his stubbed snout causes Slash to wonder what he must look like in this form. That brings him back to his embarrassment over his scarred face.

"Let's go," Zeke growls from a mouth that no longer manipulates human speech perfectly.

Slash swings his snout in the direction of the Victorian mansion, scenting Adrianna through the water as she showers.

Guards, both Singer and Were, pepper the front of the grand home. The lone fang, Brynn, accompanies them.

Determining Adrianna is safe, Slash nods at Zeke. Then they race to the edges of the hundred-acre property.

Running the perimeter is the final pursuit of security before each night falls.

Slash can't rest until he knows both his own wolves and his adopted group are safe. Then, and only then, will he lay down his weapons, eat, and clean up.

Slash blurs through the scenery, his powerful arms punching the lone branch as it sweeps forward to snap at him. Leaves and forest debris pad his swift gait. A fallen old-growth log feeds the saplings that are nourished from its rich decay. He leaps over the belly of bark and wood rot with ease, his keen eyes at Zeke's back as he travels just ahead.

Roads form a crude square around the property. Two parallel side roads run like wide railroad tracks that flank the sides of the land and Highway 101 claims the forward section.

101 is exactly where they were all picked up by Tom Harriet and his immoral pack of Reds. The only Singer spared was the aura reader, Angela.

Not a single Combatant remains alive, though Scott and Lucius are unaccounted for.

Zeke stops so abruptly, Slash all but slams into him. He evades him by inches, rolling into a half-executed somersault and catching his forward momentum with an outstretched arm against a small tree trunk. It bends then breaks, flinging Slash through the undergrowth. He slows and barrels into a massive tree trunk.

Pine needles rain down, and the scent of the forest is thick in his nose. He breathes, and they choke him. Slash ungracefully spits them out and glares at Zeke.

Zeke holds out his palm, his talons still short from his change to wolfen. Slash slaps his palm inside Zeke's and rises.

"Thanks for the warning." Slash glares, baring his teeth.

"If you smelled what I did, your ass would've puckered too."

Slash ignores him, flaring his nostrils hard.

No. *It can't be.*

He turns back to Zeke, who shrugs.

"When was the last time you scented a Lanarre?"

Slash awkwardly folds his arms, and sap causes them to stick together. He casts a sharp glance at Zeke. "Since whelphood."

"That's right." Zeke nods, his burnt orange downy hairs making him look vaguely on fire. "I can't say I *ever* have."

It's instinct. A Were knows Lycan royalty.

"Female," Zeke says, and Slash nods.

"Scenting a Lanarre in this area doesn't make a great deal of sense," Slash growls. "They're always under guard. They're pure Were, from which we all come."

Zeke shrugs. "They all take a shit every day like the rest of us. Nothing special."

Slash's lips pull into a grim smile. "It might be a little more than toilet habits, Zeke."

"A female doesn't pose a threat, and I don't smell wounds. I say we leave her be."

Slash cups his chin, fur mashing down under his hand, and slowly shakes his head. "I don't think so. A female out in this rural area is illogical. They lock down their females. No. I say we investigate and make sure she isn't in danger, then we leave it be."

"Fine, but it could be a can of worms." Greenish-gold orbs slowly spin, revolving slightly faster with Zeke's emotions.

Slash chuckles, dropping his hand. "I don't know about the Alaska dens, but when is it *not* a can of worms?"

"I don't scent any males."

"True," Zeke says. His chin lifts as he gazes at the dying sun. "Let's do it quickly and get back to One. I could eat the ass out of a hippo."

"Nice choice of words."

"Do you feel less hungry?"

Slash didn't. He thought he could eat the asses out of an entire herd. "No. I'm starved, too. The wolfen form is a bitch to maintain for this length of time. It sucks energy."

"That's in short supply," Zeke finishes.

Slash leads the way this time, scrapes and bruises from his rough landing repair and fade as he makes the steep climb toward the highway.

Tessa

So much better, Tessa sighs mentally as her urine stream finally ends. She's had to pee like a Russian race horse for the last hour.

She smirks at her ladylike thoughts while using a napkin from the last gas station to wipe. She tosses the napkin to the ground and kicks leaves over it. A pang of guilt spurs her to help mother nature in its pursuit to return everything to the earth.

Tessa scans the deep gloom of the forest. Her eyes rise up the small incline to where the car sits on the soft shoulder of Highway 101.

"Tahlia," Tessa softly calls.

"Yes," she answers.

Tessa's shoulders drop. She can't believe how fast she feels responsible for the Lanarre female.

Tessa needs that like she needs a hole in the head.

It's not enough that Tramack is up her ass, sniffing around for a good place to dry hump her leg. *No-oh, I've got to take in a stray Were female.* Not any Were female, but a Lanarre princess.

Dumb, Tessa. Really dumb.

It is what it is.

"Come here."

Tahlia moves between two huge fir trees. She's so quiet, Tessa's not sure if she would hear her had she not been directly in front of her and within sight.

"You're quiet."

"Stealth movement is a very important part of my training."

Tessa cocks an eyebrow. "This is so weird. Really. Forgive me, but if you're this important princess—"

Tahlia folds her arms, looking very close to a rant.

Ignoring her, Tessa goes on, "Then why teach you all this combat stuff?"

"I am female, nonetheless—I have skills the Lanarre wish to develop. Not one Lanarre's importance is ignored. Whatever aptitude they possess is built upon, harnessed."

"Uh-huh," Tessa says.

Tahlia releases her arms and shrugs. "I'm not making this up. The Lanarre feels responsible for all Were. We must be *excellent* in all things. Otherwise, we're unworthy of the title of ruler of the Lycan."

Oh, moon.

"So what happened?"

Tahlia's eyes lower, and she presses her beat-up sneaker into the moss, making a tread indentation. "We cannot be responsible for all wrongdoing or for all Were falling away from the principles of Lycan."

Tahlia's head jerks up, and she plants her legs far apart, fists ready and loose at her side. She morphs from delicate to fierce in seconds.

Tessa turns around slowly and sights two Were, both in wolfen form.

"Stay behind me, Tahlia," Tessa warns, her voice low.

"I am a better forward fighter," she comments casually. Tessa turns to tell her what's what.

She is gone.

Tessa feels the breeze over her head and as Tahlia flings herself over Tessa's head.

"No!" Tessa screams and charges the males.

Tahlia lands in front of a seven-foot-tall Were whose deeply scarred face has the most tender hard eyes Tessa has ever seen.

He's seen too much, is Tessa's lone thought before Tahlia launches herself at the other Were male.

Tahlia's hand is a blur.

She steps away from that Were and moves in on the scarred one.

"Forgive me," he says in the heavily graveled voice of the wolfen form then hits Tahlia at the side of her neck.

She falls in a silent heap.

The other Were is on his knees, four trails where talons swiped across his throat bleeding.

His esophagus shines like a slick cream worm in his throat.

Tessa moves in before the scarred Were can hurt Tahlia more. The girl is already coming around.

Their eyes meet from her prone position, and she kicks her leg up, narrowly missing the scarred one's nutsack.

Holy moon, this is so bad.

Tessa hits him full speed, and he grabs her forearm, spinning her off behind him with her own momentum.

Tessa lands on her ass with a hard thump. Her wind is gone, and she lies on her back, unable to breathe.

I have to change. Like yesterday.

Tessa's body shifts to the quarter-change seamlessly, and her lungs fill. They're just slightly bigger, better, and more proficient at oxygen intake.

Tahlia is pinned against the scarred Were, her back to his front.

"Don't hurt her. She is Lanarre," Tessa says as a last resort. She's not sure what these males know about the species. Her own knowledge was pretty inadequate. But if they know anything, they know not to fuck with the Lanarre—ever.

"We know," the scarred Were says. "We are not here to harm, but to help."

"Could've said," Tessa replies as the deepening gloom tests her improved vision. She does manage to make out that he is Alpha—and a Red. There's no hiding that sunset-colored fur.

"This one didn't give us the chance. My second heals a grievous wound."

Tessa rolls her eyes. Tahlia's wide eyes are on hers. "He'll live, and my moon, don't you know better than to sneak up on two females?"

His face shows surprise.

"Don't look at me like that, Red. We were out here taking a tinkle, and you guys sidle up? Moon help us."

He scowls. "If I let you go, are you going to give me a new blow hole?" the scarred one asks.

"What? Are you a whale?" Tahlia asks in a sulk.

Tessa laughs.

The other Were is on his hands and knees, massaging his throat. "That fucking *hurt*."

Tahlia harrumphs, and the injured Were glares at her.

"What pack are you from?" Tessa asks tersely.

"I won't harm you," Tahlia says.

The scarred Were backs away so quickly that Tessa can't track the movement, even in her quarter-change form.

"I'm Slash, from the Southeastern."

Tessa can't hide her relief.

Slash frowns at her curiously. "I take it that's a good thing."

She nods a little too quickly. "A very good thing."

"Tramack from the Western hunts me."

"You're rogue?" the injured Were asks, standing, the surprise evident in his voice.

The furrows from Tahlia's expert swipe fully close, and the skin remains shiny with fresh scar tissue.

"Are you going to judge?"

His eyes glitter at her. "Not yet." But his gaze shifts to Tahlia.

"We are here to help. We can't do that when you attack us," Slash explains logically.

Tessa puts her hands on her hips. "We are female."

"Clearly," the other Were says. His lips pull into a sardonic tilt, and he performs a little bow, though the cough from his abused throat ruins the effect. "I'm Zeke."

"Well here's the thing, *Zeke*. Tramack of the Western is hunting me and has declared me his intended. There's a bounty on my head, and he means to collect me. This Lanarre's human guardians were slaughtered by a rogue male that I should have killed. She was traveling to…" Tessa looks at Tahlia, wondering how much she should say.

Tahlia nods. "Go ahead. It is fine that anyone knows."

"Tahlia is traveling to mate her chosen."

Both males look at Tahlia. "She doesn't look old enough to mate."

Tahlia kicks up her chin. "I am of age."

Slash snorts in the background, and Tahlia gives him her best dirty look, which Tessa thinks is quite good.

Zeke thumbs his chin thoughtfully, running the digit back and forth across the downy bright-red fur. He's handsome.

He's also Red. Tessa's running for her life without a plan.

I don't need a male.

When she looks up, his thoughtful glance has narrowed to her face. His nostrils flare once, and he smirks.

The insufferable pig. Tessa fumes, thinking he might have guessed her mild interest as she fights to behave casually.

Slash spreads his arms away from his body. "We can offer you temporary shelter and protection until you figure out what you want to do."

Tahlia looks her age as she rolls her lip between her teeth, indecision painted on every plane of her face. "The Lanarre will look for me."

Her eyes slide to Slash then land accusingly on Zeke.

Slash's brows draw together. "And you will be under our protection."

"You are a stubborn female," Zeke says to Tahlia.

"You have no idea," Tessa mutters, thinking about their brief acquaintance.

Tahlia frowns at her.

"It's true!" Tessa defends.

Instead of answering, Tahlia leads the way, heading in the direction from where the Were popped up.

Tahlia gives Tessa the barest smile as she walks by, as if she holds a secret.

10

Julia

*J*ulia has been dirty before. But after being bit, beaten, and bruised, a shower has never felt so good. She dries off and carefully combs through hair, which hasn't seen a brush in a couple of days. Julia tosses on a T, jeans, and shoes that don't aggravate her feet, which are still healing from the cross-country trek.

The few hours since they arrived with the Region Two Singers were not easy ones.

The Were are complaining that the grounds feel like a graveyard. Their acute sense of smell picks up every single thing. Every death. Every wound.

That stirs an idea. Julia can't discern one dead body from another. But it's critical that she know if Victor is dead. *And what of Reagan and Delilah?*

Then there's Tharell. He claimed he was instructed to deceive the Singers—and ultimately betray William—and, ruled by the black blood of the demonic, he had no other choice. He broke his pact with the Northwestern coven by not delivering Julia to them.

Gabriel, Julia's mind whispers, then on the heels of that name, Julia remembers Claire. A longing for Claire swamps her, as does a yearning for William. He was deeply self-contained. As it turns out, he was her ultimate protector.

Julia is sitting by herself in the room she's occupied since the first day she arrived at Region One. The cracked doorknob and hole in the wall stand in testimony to tempers—attacks.

Now everything's different. Jen, Michael, and Brendan are gone.

Scott.

A silent tear files its slow way over her still-warm skin from her shower. It plops on top of her tightly knitted fingers.

She'll never hear a wise-ass Michael belittle someone with his scathing sarcasm in between lollipop licks. Julia won't listen to the sibling fights Jen adored stirring up.

Brendan won't be making any more manure piles or phantom holes for the stray vamp to fall into.

They were sort of a family; the only one she had. When all hope was lost and she thought Jason was dead, they were there for her in a way only Jason and Cyn had been.

Julia hiccups, and a sob pops out like a bubble of sadness. It bursts in the silent room, filling the space with her loss.

Now her family is Jason, Cyn, and Jacqueline—of all people.

Julia slowly raises her head and plops her chin in her hand. There *is* her hidden sister in Alaska. But for now, the people who remain—the Singers—will need her.

Julia stands at the edge of the bed. After wetting a cold washcloth and blotting her tear-streaked face, she makes her way downstairs.

The kitchen is filled with women and a few industrious guys, making great-smelling food. Dishes being clanked and set out for people are the noises of comfort and gathering.

Saliva pools inside her mouth, and Julia realizes she hasn't eaten in twenty-four hours.

Jacqueline sits at the table, one hand on her belly, her chin perched on her fist.

Cyn stares at Jacqueline with clear suspicion.

Julia smiles. *Some things remain the same.*

"Jules!" Cyn cries, running to her. Julia has seconds to see that Cyn has somehow styled her hair, and is wearing cute clothes before she hurls herself in Julia's arms. They dance in a circle and finally Cyn releases her.

"So happy you're finally done wallowing in the shower. I thought you were setting up camp. Is there any hot water left?"

Julia blinks.

Cyn frowns.

"Hello. Maybe you need more sleep?"

"On-demand hot water heater," Jason says, walking into the kitchen and pressing a light kiss on her forehead. Julia glances up, grateful for his presence. He squeezes her shoulder, and Julia still feels as if she's in some kind of shock-induced fog. Julia's hand comes to rest on her stomach, where she was stabbed.

"Food time," Jason says, striking his palm against his washboard abs. He jerks open the fridge door, hangs on the top, and juts his face forward like a pecking hen.

Julia walks over there and pulls the fridge door out of his grasp. She shuts it, opens it, then shuts it again.

Jason's brows come together, and he retreats a step. "Babe, what are ya doing?"

Julia sucks in her lower lip. "Michael said the key to finding food in the fridge was to look three times."

The room falls silent.

Julia bursts into tears.

"Come here, babe," Jason pulls her into his arms and she sobs against his broad shoulder.

Again.

"Let 'em go, baby. Let 'em go."

Julia sniffs, wiping her tears against his hard chest. "Sorry," she says, shaking her head, her damp hair making him wet where her tears don't. "I'm having a hard time still."

"That's okay. It'll take time."

A big commotion of voices burst all around them, and Julia looks up.

Beaten and torn, Scott staggers into the kitchen.

Without thinking, Julia runs to Scott. He gives her a weary smile.

His lips are cut, one eye is swollen shut, and a deep open wound bisects the other eyebrow.

"Julia," he croaks, and she wraps her arms around his waist.

"Ah!" she cries as they begin to topple like a clumsy, half-cut tree, and Julia stumbles under his weight.

"Come on, Hulk. Don't crush the queen, pal." Jason puts a hand underneath his arm and scoops the larger man to an upright position.

Cyn walks slowly toward them. Her eyes meet Julia's, and she gives a small shake of her head.

Julia looks down and sees Scott's femur gleaming like a fanged tooth hanging from his upper thigh.

"Heal him," Jacqueline says from behind Cyn.

Cyn turns, hands on hips. "You're still bossy. And y'know? I think I wouldn't be if I were in your position. Like I wouldn't dig in and get it figured out and stuff."

Jacqueline just stares.

"Gah!" Cyn says. "Fine, but this is going to be a hold-him-down moment."

Jason guides a limping Scott to the flowered fainting couch in the front parlor and carefully lays him down. Scott's skin is chalky with a green cast.

Julia moves to his side, drops to her knees, and grabs his hand. He winces.

She looks down and sees he's completely missing two fingernails.

"Oh, my God, Scott!" Julia cries, covering her mouth with the hand that's not holding his. "What did they do to you?"

Scott licks his dry lips. One beautiful, dark eye rolls to meet Julia's. "Less than they did to Lucius."

Julia's shoulders shake with her effort to be strong. This is what a leader has to deal with, these cold facts. But more tears come, collecting at her jaw and dampening the thin long-sleeved T-shirt she's wearing.

"Where is Lucius?" Angela asks quietly as she steps up behind Julia.

She didn't hear.

Scott's gaze meets Angela's over Julia's shoulder. He closes his eyes, and Angela cries out, rushing from the room.

"Okay, boys, hold stud-boy down while I set this break."

Julia's eyes hold Cyn's. "Are you—do you know what you're doing?"

She smiles, shaking her head. "Hell, no. But my hands do."

That'll have to be good enough.

Cyn's expression goes serious. "Take a hike, Jules. You're not gonna like the noise he makes."

"It's okay, Julia," Scott says.

Julia leans forward to kiss his forehead, but can't find an uninjured area.

Scott squeezes her hand, trying to comfort her.

She covers her ears when Scott begins to scream.

Julia doesn't leave or look away from his uninjured eye.

His screams fall blissfully silent when he passes out from the pain.

Praile

Praile's wounds weep and fester underneath the ill-fitting human clothes. Further, he must expend an inordinate amount of energy to maintain some form of camouflage.

He must expend more precious energy than Lazarus, who has only a tail and a minor bit of skin cover to effect. His eyes, teeth, and even his nails fall within acceptable appearance for a human male. How Lazarus manages to look so undemonic is a mystery. *Genes—always a crapshoot, as the humans say.*

"Hide the bodies," Praile commands the two low demons who accompanied him and Lazarus. Hardly more than drones, they can take only one form.

Praile has chosen homeless men. It is a little bit of an inside joke, but he must take the small doses of humor when they present themselves. They're like medicine, especially of late.

If Praile uses his ability to see things through his human eyes, he sees how the demonics would appear to humans.

Lazarus will appear handsome.

Praile grunts as the low demons drag the old couple out of their respective car seats and into the woods.

An age-old trick. Well, not entirely. The tactic is as old as cars, and those have been in existence for just over a hundred years. However, it's been very handy to lie in the center of the road and appear helpless.

That had been Lazarus's job. Praile was unwilling to re-open wounds that were healing badly.

He is ecstatic the Master cannot access his thoughts. If he could, Praile would be dead twice over. Everything he has thought since the thirteenth lash has been of the most evil and vile variety.

His thoughts have been especially uncharitable toward the Master.

Lazarus says nothing, cradling his hand, which he broke while stopping the car that last inch.

"That'll set wrong," Praile says, stating the obvious.

"Yes," Lazarus reluctantly agrees through his teeth.

Praile doesn't smile but marginally contains how pleased he is to see the stoic Lazarus feel pain. After all, he is not healing Praile fully. Praile doesn't care that the Master has tasked Lazarus with doing a partial healing—he still blames his second.

The two low demons return to the soft shoulder, hunched and mindless as the bees he thought of earlier.

"Good," Praile says. "Get in the back."

The two slouch inside the back of the car. Lazarus slides behind the steering wheel and just sits there.

"What are you doing?" Praile bites out.

Then he spies a sliver of bone that has punched through the inside and lower part of Lazarus's wrist. Though demonics are brutally strong, the car *was* going around fifty miles per hour.

"I can set it," Lazarus says.

Praile grins then winces as his back touches the seat. He jerks upright, glancing at Lazarus. His face is expressionless, as usual. In fact, Praile doesn't find proof of pain except for a certain tightness about his eyes.

"But you can't heal the injury?"

"No."

Praile know of no demonic or healer who can heal themselves. They heal only others.

"Too bad," Praile sings falsely, smoothing his hands down the stiff denim of his jeans. He lets his form go while he's hidden in the car, and a sigh escapes him.

Lazarus puts the car in gear with his good hand, and makes his way toward the region where Praile has been told the Angelic Blood has gathered. The High One will be his in the next day—or lashes will be the least of his concern.

11

Slash

Slash is ready.

Ready to be done. Ready to see Adrianna. He doesn't want two antagonistic females to babysit. He wants one female forever.

Slash is usually more focused on the task at hand. When openings for security detail came up, he and Zeke were the first to volunteer.

Then the impossible happened. A Lanarre female stumbled into the equation.

Slash's eyes move to Tessa, the older of the two. Her thick black hair is plaited in a single braid down her broad back. It's easy to see she's female, but there's not a soft spot anywhere on her athletic frame. Her wide gray eyes are framed by sooty lashes that match her hair. A dusky complexion contrasts to a smattering of freckles over her straight nose.

The freckles reminds him of Adrianna, and his heart beats harder.

As is the norm, both females have a healthy dose of prejudice against him and Zeke.

That makes sense, because nothing good circulates about the Reds. Alaska is overrun with Reds, and they don't behave like a proper den. Instead, they run in immature, un-led packs, selecting mates indiscriminately. They've given all Reds everywhere a bad name.

Zeke keeps a watchful eye on the young female, as he should. She's shown a prowess for self-defense atypical of female Weres, though Alpha females are known for their contentious streak.

Slash grins.

Tahlia notices and asks what's so funny.

"Nothing is funny. I'm thinking about how interesting it will be for you to meet Adrianna."

Her faces screws up into a frown.

Zeke covers a smile with a cough and Tessa, appearing more jaded than all of them, looks between the two males and narrows her eyes.

"I know you're not going to hurt us," she begins, and Zeke's expressive face gives him away.

Tessa stops hiking and crosses her arms. "Listen, I already told you. Two females are alone, then two wolfen males pop up like jack-in-the-Weres *and* don't let us know if they're friends…"

"We obviously assume you are foes," Tahlia says with a touch of arrogance in her voice.

Zeke glowers but says, "Obviously. Hated the talon swipe. Hurts like a bitch. Heals like hell."

Slash chuckles. Zeke rolls with circumstances—a critical component to surviving in their supernatural reality.

"Anyway," Tessa drawls, "that doesn't mean I don't need any background about where we'll be taking temporary shelter. What is expected of us?"

Another full look passes between him and Zeke.

"Okay, who stepped on your puppy?" Tessa asks.

Tahlia looks around.

"I don't see any dogs." Then she smirks, giving a significant look at the two males in wolfen form.

"It's an expression," Tessa says with a proper amount of impatience.

Zeke scowls at Tahlia. "You speak your opinion without any fear of reprisal."

Tahlia clasps her hands behind her back. "And you *can* speak. I was beginning to wonder."

Their stares clash, and Zeke marches over to Tahlia. She tilts her face upward.

An expression of panic washes over Tessa's face.

Tahlia's either stupid or brave.

Or both.

Zeke is a foot and a half taller than Tahlia is. He looms over her, and with a low growl, he moves as though to speak.

Tahlia tips her head back, exposing the smooth skin of her throat to Zeke. "You would harm me because of my sharp tongue?" she whispers.

Zeke sways forward, as if he's in a dreamlike state. "Not harm—no."

He grips her shoulders and sinks his short snout into the crook of her neck, letting out a low growl.

The posturing has gone on long enough.

"Do something," Tessa says, and Slash sprints the short distance to the pair.

Zeke's snout comes away from her neck, and she sinks against him, sliding her arms around his waist.

Fuck.

His eyes spin like emerald fire at Slash, but the revolutions are too fast to track. "Keep your distance."

Slash tenses. "Let the Lanarre go."

Her defiant gaze moves to Slash. "I do not wish to."

"Tahlia," Tessa warns, "this is dangerous."

Zeke presses his snout against Tahlia's hair, scenting deeply of her.

"She nearly decapitated you," Slash says.

Zeke ignores him.

Slash exhales in disgust. "You're drunk from her scent. Step away."

Zeke growls in challenge. Slash has no desire to injure or kill his newest second.

He gives the Lanarre the contemptuous look she deserves.

Tahlia sniffs at him. "Do not look down on me, Red."

Slash folds his arms as his second rolls in her scent. Zeke's snout disappears underneath her hair, and he only comes up for air to press his nose in another unscented spot.

"He is a good Were. Do not charm him."

Tahlia smiles. "Shall I charm you?"

"Won't work, whelp. You're too young, I'm too pure, and I have a female."

Tahlia pouts, and the expression makes her look even younger than she is. She plays childish games with dangerous players.

Grudgingly, she loosens her hold on Zeke and steps away. He tries to follow.

"Zeke!" Slash says in a sharp voice.

The Were's head jerks. He shakes it as though he were asleep. In a way, he was.

The Lanarre placed at the pinnacle of their species is a danger. With other lesser Were, they are treacherous. Zeke's mixed heritage make him vulnerable to her compulsions.

Zeke gazes at Tahlia. Slash watches his expression change from one of dumb thrall, as he's seen a human look at a vamp, to one of anger. "That is not right."

Tahlia shrugs. "It's important you know with whom you deal."

"Where is the selfless girl that saved my life?" Tessa asks with a touch of sadness in her voice.

Tahlia's expression hardens. "I will not be ruled by males. Or anyone. My chosen, Drek—he is the only male who stands over me. I am Lanarre."

Tessa makes a sound of distaste. "Well, good for you. I am a rogue Alpha who's been followed for two decades by a packmaster who doesn't care how I feel—that I think independently at all." Her eyes bore into Tahlia's. "But I'm not going to do a catnip routine on all males because of one male."

Amen to that. Slash enjoys Tessa's spirit. "Catnip?"

Zeke chuckles. "I like you," he says to Tessa.

"Thanks, but don't get any ideas."

Slash laughs and turns to walk back toward Region One.

"How much longer?" Tahlia asks after an awkward silent ten minutes of marching through the woods.

Very young.

"We'll be there when we get there."

Whelps.

Julia

She spots them first, which is amazing, considering all the others in the group have eyesight better than hers.

Julia jogs out to meet Slash and Zeke.

She takes in the two women who they're walking with. Julia doesn't miss the healing talon marks at Zeke's throat, either.

Jason is there before she can open her mouth, his arm straying in front of her. "Whoa, babe. Let's see what's what."

Of course, he's right, but Julia's emotional upkeep is taking its toll. She doesn't *want* to follow rules or keep how she feels silent. Scott has returned.

Her people are dead.

Julia badly wants to be in charge of her destiny. And she will be if it's the last thing she does.

"Don't baby me, Jason," Julia says, scooting around his arm.

He sighs.

"Uh-huh, 'cause you're not a danger magnet or some such shit?"

Julia ignores him, and Slash, who's normally quiet, pipes up, "These are some stray Were we picked up on our perimeter sweep." He jerks a thumb at the young women behind him.

Julia stares openly.

A couple of years ago, she would have made a stab at being polite. Three years in the supernatural world has all but scrubbed away the human niceties.

The younger one is striking. Her large wide-set eyes have the barest almond shape and an almost violet hue. Dark ringlets spiral out and away from her face, overwhelming her slim body. Her nose is straight; her lips, full.

They look fuller for the pouting.

It makes her look about twelve, though Julia is pretty good at guessing age, and she thinks the girl is closer to twenty. But if she's Were, that could be way off. Julia's gaze latches on to the older woman. Her long hair is as dark as night, and her startling gray eyes are not light as Victor's were. They are the color of a coming storm.

She meets Julia's stare unblinkingly.

Alpha for sure.

"I'm Julia," she says with a smile.

"Tessa," the young woman replies.

The younger introduces herself as Tahlia.

She has some kind of accent, which Julia can't pinpoint.

"I'm sure that Slash and Zeke didn't bring you back here because everything's all hunky-dory."

Tessa grins suddenly, and the expression softens her face. "No, you've got that right. But I'll be honest."

Well, thank heaven for that.

"I don't want to bring what I've got chasing me down on you guys." Her worried eyes fall on Julia.

Julia frowns. *Nope, Region One sure doesn't need any more bad crap.* But she won't turn away defenseless women.

Her eyes stray to Zeke's neck. *Maybe not so defenseless.*

Jason's strong hands move to Julia's shoulders. "Up to you."

Isn't it always?

Tessa's expression is neutral and Julia can't read Tahlia's.

"You're welcome to stay here if you don't mind a little work." Julia's mouth twists. "Or a lot."

Tessa's shoulders drop, and she lets out a sigh of obvious relief. Julia turns to Tahlia, who looks untroubled. Her deep poise is weird for somebody so young, and Julia is very interested to hear why a young female Were is away from her den. It makes zero sense. Julia remembers how closely they guarded her when she was at the Northwestern den.

Julia steps forward and shakes hands with the women. The constant chattering white noise inside her brain intensifies unmercifully for a moment then subsides. She takes a shaky breath and smiles, despite the ESP distraction.

Being a telepath can be a liability. And when it comes to the Were, it's like bad noise that fills her head and makes it hurt.

"You okay?" Jason asks in a low voice, and Tessa's ears perk.

Julia nods, rubbing her temples. "Yeah." She shakes off the disquieting telepathic current. "I bet you guys are hungry?" she asks, taking the focus off herself.

"Starved," Tessa admits with a grateful smile.

"I could eat," Tahlia says.

"Great, follow me." Julia turns around and without waiting for anyone, makes her way back to the kitchen.

The guilt is there, but Julia ignores it. She wants to see Scott.

She's pulled to him like a moth to a flame. Though the soul-meld was wiped out in faerie, Julia wonders if something still remains.

It's possible the tie is the reason why she never really grieved when Tom Harriet took him. Julia must've known, deep down, that he was still alive.

And she's glad. Julia's married to Jason, but she's happy Scott's alive and that he's here.

Her feelings are still kind of a mess.

Julia gets the women settled and moves quietly through the mansion without a guide, until she reaches a closed door on the second floor. She's never been inside this room before. The house is over seven thousand square feet, probably closer to eight. There are two dozen rooms, nine bedrooms and six bathrooms.

Scott could be anywhere.

She lays the flat of her palm on the polished wood door. Her every sense has come alive and they're raw.

"Come in, Julia," Scott says.

She sighs and turns the crystal knob, swinging the door wide.

Scott's propped up on pillows.

Julia doesn't speak to the weirdness between them. Instead, she asks about something safe. "How's the leg?"

Scott shrugs. "It'll be good soon."

Julia looks at her feet. "How soon?" When she looks up, Scott's right in front of her. In. Front. Of. Her.

Julia jerks her chin back. "What—what are you doing? How'd you move that fast?"

Scott doesn't say anything. His hand moves to her shoulder and floats down to her wrist, then his fingers twine with hers.

The breath she's been holding slides out in defeat. She forgot Scott is so tall, so big—and so terribly dangerous.

But he's not dangerous to her, never to her.

His injured eye has healed enough to open, and his dark gaze finds hers. His hand moves to her jaw, and he feathers his thumb along its edge.

"Did you believe what Tharell told you?"

She didn't expect the question. Julia shakes her head because she can't think. She's numb with what his touch means. Inert like unshaped clay.

This can't be happening. Julia was so sure she had it figured out. That her path was set.

Scott grasps her chin, moving it gently so their eyes lock. "That a soul-meld could be thrown away because we were in a faerie mound?" His voice is rife with disbelief. "What in the hell did he think would happen once we left?" Scott's brows come together at the apparent obviousness of it all.

"I guess..." Julia tries to retreat from his embrace, and it's like stepping out of warm bathwater into a cold bathroom.

I don't want to go.

"I assumed…"

Scott's eyebrows jam tighter. "Uh-huh. You know what they say about assuming."

Julia makes an inarticulate noise as he buries his fingers in her hair. He makes a fist, twisting the tendrils, creating a sensation just shy of true pain.

"It makes an ass," he whispers against her temple, "out of you…"

He kisses her there, and she whimpers, "And me."

Then his lips are on hers, and Julia forgets she's married to another man or that Scott's been tortured by an insane Were.

The wet heat of his kiss is all that exists in the entire universe. And the soul-meld locks into place once more, as if it never left.

Julia should mourn its return.

But when the soul's other piece has found its mate, there is no grief—only joy.

12

Praile

*L*azarus pulls up behind a vintage 1960s vehicle and parks.

Good era, Praile remembers. *So much simpler to sway the innocent then.* Now humanity is so cynical, he can hardly take pleasure in showing the masses the path to Hades. Happily, many are already on a one-way course.

Lazarus inhales deeply. He rolled down the driver's window as they slowed. "Were. Female." He closes his eyes. "Two."

Praile frowns. Those are not the words he was hoping to hear. Praile swings the car door open and winces as the material of his shirt tears away from his wounds

Fucking lashes.

Gravel crunches under his stiff running shoes as he walks around to the passenger-side door. The car has fins near the trunk and has been well-preserved.

Curiously, it's abandoned.

Praile does not believe in coincidence of any kind. He pops open the door and peers inside.

"What's happened here?" he fires at Lazarus.

His bright-blue gaze pins Praile from across the seat as he leans in opposite him. Praile has always known of Lazarus's hate for him, but he is oh-so-careful about letting it manifest visibly.

"Give me a moment, and I will try to discern what's happened."

The thread of irritation buried in that neutral voice pleases Praile.

"I wish to determine where the High One's hidey-hole is."

Lazarus gives a mild exhale of utter irritation.

"Problem, Lazarus?"

His eyes shift away, and Praile knows the movement makes it more difficult for Praile to read emotion. *Clever demon.*

"No."

Liar. Praile's nostrils flare, smelling the untruth.

Lazarus holds up a palm. "I am aware of what the end game is, Praile."

"Good. Do not lie to me again."

Lazarus says nothing. His eyes close, and he inhales in short chuffs. Finally, his eyelids sweep open, icy-blue irises blazing.

"One female is a Lanarre."

Praile whistles, delighted at the revelation. Then his eyebrows drop. He palms his chin with undisguised talons. "What is Lycan royalty doing cavorting about?"

Lazarus shrugs. "It's not important, really. What *is*—is the women marked their territory and left this fine stolen vehicle behind."

Praile swivels his head to Lazarus in a hard glance of interest. "Really?"

Lazarus nods. "Really. And two Red Weres accompany them."

"Fantastic," Praile breathes out reverently. "This is wonderful news."

Lazarus's lips lift.

Praile waves his palm around. "You know what I mean."

"I do." Lazarus frowns suddenly. "Why are you not maintaining your form?"

It's not as easy for me, fool.

Of course, Lazarus is no fool and gives him a knowing look.

Praile shrugs. "I will slip my human shield on when we near Region One. I only need to employ it for a short time. The Angelic who remain will not know of our deceit if we're not in our true from."

In battle, the demonic must be in their true form. In all other things, the parody of humanity is perfect.

Praile sighs. "To know that the High One and the blood babe are finally here after all this time." Praile's gaze spears Lazarus and he gives a smug nod.

"The world is our oyster, Lazarus."

Lazarus is silent. And that silence suits Praile. He mainly enjoys listening to himself. He needs no other audience.

They lock both cars and walk into the woods. Praile knows everything will soon be within reach, even the swollen promises made by the Master.

Julia

"Scott!" Julia shoves him away, freaking.

He's been tortured and has a broken leg.

She's all sorts of miserable.

He laughs.

"Oh, my God." Her voice trembles, and she puts her shaking hand over her scorched lips. "*So* not funny."

Scott sobers. "Sorry. I guess I'm just a little fucking giddy about surviving Harriet's treatment, escaping and coming back here to you."

His hand finds her nape and applies a tender squeeze.

Julia moans. "This is so bad. You can't be happy to come back to me. There is no us."

"No," he whispers. "It's so good—right."

He leans down and peppers kisses on her forehead. His hot lips move to each eyelid, and she feels his eyelashes brush against her own.

"And my asshole brothers. I was actually beginning to miss those guys," Scott says softly with a smile in his voice.

It's cold water on all Julia's senses.

Scott doesn't know about his father. Brendan, Jen—Michael.

Oh no.

Scott watches emotions run across her face, fleeing for safety from his perceptive gaze.

His fingers tighten on her shoulders, sensing her morbidity. "What the hell has you looking at me like that?" Dark eyes pull at her, and Julia's drowning in all that deep brown.

Lightheadedness swims close.

"Julia, I'm sorry." Scott drags her over to the bed and gently lays her down.

She notices his slight limp and smells the soap he's used since his return.

What's wrong with me?

He takes both her hands. "Now tell me what's happening?"

"You noticed we don't have many people?"

"Ah, *no.* I noticed we have an assload of Region Two Singers. And let's face it. Observation skills were on the down low." His gaze moves over Julia's face, coming to rest on her eyes.

Scott stands up, realization making swift work of his face. "Dad?"

Julia doesn't look away.

She counts it as the hardest thing she's ever done. "I don't have a good way to tell you."

His expression morphs to granite, and he touches the top of her head lightly to take the sting out of his words. "Spit it out."

"He's gone, Scott. Tony killed him."

"Tony? The apeshit Were that tortured *my*—Jacqueline?"

Julia nods miserably. "Yeah," she answers softly.

Scott slowly lowers himself to the bed and puts his face in his hands. A full minute pounds by silently.

He rolls his face in his hands to look at her. The bruises are already fading, but they're gruesome splashes of dying yellow on his skin. "I'm not ready for this shit."

Julia sits up, feels like puking, swallows, and plows forward. "What shit?"

Scott gives a wan smile. "If he's gone, I am the head of Region One. Only royal blood can rule. And—" He clears his throat. "He will be missed. I can't believe he's gone."

They stare at each other.

Scott's face changes as the wheels of his fine mind turn, no doubt thinking about what it would mean if Marcus were gone. She see when he realizes her omission, and that his siblings are absent from the mansion.

"Don't tell me, Julia."

Julia's tears don't even burn to warn her. Like escaped convicts, they run down her face, away from the prison of her eyes, then conspire together at her collarbone.

She cries for them both, and it's still not enough.

"What happened? What the fuck happened to my family?" He cups his large hand at the back of her head, keeping a grip on her nape.

Julia begins speaking.

When she's done, there's a void in her that wasn't there before.

Julia recognizes it for what it is—that part of Scott that she owns, just as he owns a piece of her.

He's empty, and now, so is she.

So empty.

"Do you want something to eat?" Julia finally asks.

Scott shakes his head.

Julia puts a hand over her stomach. It still hurts. She looks at Scott.

"I feel your hunger under all this." Julia waves her hand around, symbolically encompassing all the weighted grief that's been aired between them.

"Maybe," Scott replies ruefully. "But who cares about the hole in your gut when the one in your heart's twice as big? Who gives a fat fuck?" he yells.

Julia yelps in surprise, scooting back from him.

Scott picks up the nearest thing and hurls it into the wall. Then he throws another. Glass shatters and flies. Shards embed themselves into whatever they can.

One spears Julia's palm as she hides behind her hands.

She hears a gasp but doesn't move. Julia rides out his justified rage in a safe spot against the headboard of the bed.

"Oh, Julia, I'm sorry," he says, plucking out the glass.

A teardrop of blood wells from her palm.

His eyes are bright with his sorrow. His cheekbones flame with the blood pumping so freely with the river of his anger.

"It's okay," she whispers.

"No, I—let me heal this."

Scott breathes over her hand and the blood stops flowing. He kisses the center of the wound and it begins to close.

"Oh, wow...wow."

"It's a bennie," Scott says.

"It's real, isn't it?" she asks, scared to look at his eyes for what she'll see there. She looks up anyway.

He nods. "No one can heal you beside a Singer Healer."

She swallows painfully. "And...my soul-meld."

Something occurs to Julia, something besides the new mess she currently finds herself in.

"You just made a bunch of noise."

He blows out an exhale, ripping a hand over his short hair, clearly not getting the relevance. "Yup."

"Nobody came."

Scott cocks his head. "You're right."

He stands, towing Julia with him. "You said Tony"—his chin dips, and Julia tries to notice everything but the standing water in his eyes—"killed everyone?"

Julia nods. "Well, there were a handful of Region One Singers, but…" She spreads her hands away from her body. "I'm sorry," she barely gets out.

Scott's brows knit. "I don't understand why no one hid in the bunker?" He shakes his head.

Pain flares in Julia's chest. Instant and sharp, it pierces her.

Scott grabs her. "What? What is it?"

"What bunker?" she whispers urgently.

Scott blinks slowly. "The bunker that stays vacuum-locked for seventy-two hours after entry. No one gets in. No one gets out. Period."

"Julia!" Jason yells, rushing into the room.

She turns with a guilty jump, and his eyes travel from her to Scott. They narrow, missing nothing and seeing stuff she can't explain. She doesn't want to.

Scott drops Julia's hands, and she's grateful, even though she feels as if they've been amputated without his touch.

Oh, God.

"What—" She clears her throat, barely able to meet the eyes of the man she loves—or thought she loved. "What is it?"

Jason walks to her and takes the hands Scott just dropped. "There's more survivors."

Scott says nothing. His silence speaks for him.

Jason flicks a glance Scott's way and Julia notes the chill in that hazel glance.

"Scott knows."

"Right. Well, his sister and Michael are alive. And Victor too. They were stowed away in some nuclear shelter thing."

Scott's instant grin is contagious.

Before she knows it, Julia can't wipe its twin off her face.

Jason throws an arm around Julia's shoulders. "They're prepared. I'll give them that." His hand flips up, and his fingertips curl around her shoulder. "Victor says he gathered the royalty together, and as many women and children that he could. They've been down there three days."

Julia makes a face thinking about that—but they're alive.

Jason laughs. "Don't get all grossed out, Jules. They had a bathroom, food, running water. It's a damn underground Hilton."

Scott says, "I wouldn't go that far. It has only the supplies needed for the seventy-two-hour time frame and no more."

"Still!" Jason swings his hands up, piercing Julia with his hazel gaze. "Great news, huh?" He grabs her neck and pulls her against him, pressing a gentle kiss against her forehead, right over the crescent-shaped scar.

It *is* great news.

So why do I feel so sad?

Jason keeps one of her hands and tows her out of Scott's bedroom.

Julia glances over her shoulder. Scott's lips are in a flat hard line; his eyes are fixed on their joined hands.

13

Slash

Slash is vaguely pessimistic by nature, but he would admit that seeing those Singers, twenty in all, climb out of a trapdoor in a well-hidden spot under the mansion lifted his sagging spirits. With so many Singers gone, there was no one left to alert them to the survival quarters. Scott returned, and the surprise existence of additional survivors brought levity to a grim climate.

Anthony Laurent moved through the Region One Singers, using his demonic saber like a knife through butter. Tony struck down Victor, but the Were was apparently in a rush—he missed Victor's carotid artery by a fraction. Victor laid in a pool of his blood while the Were kicked him in the balls.

Thinking about Tony makes Slash's blood boil. He would kill him again if the chance was served up.

Fortunately, he's gone, and Victor has mighty recuperative powers.

Slash had barely managed to heal himself enough to function when he saw what Tony was doing to the others. Victor cut his losses.

Cold but pragmatic, Victor headed straight to where he assumed the most important Singers would congregate. He was able to save Jen and Michael.

Slash scans the faces of those who survived. Everyone is somber, as they should be.

That's how Slash would feel if he'd listened to the screams, begging, and pleas for mercy while Tony rained death down upon their heads.

"This is so sad," Adrianna says and he takes her hand in his.

She squeezes Slash's fingers. Unfamiliar heat blooms in his chest where an emptiness was before. It hurts, though it feels right.

Slash won't discuss their evolving relationship. He can't. It'll make the hope into solid reality by speaking of it. Instead, he discusses more neutral matters. "It's better that they're alive. More Singers survived than we presumed, important ones."

He studies Julia as she greets everyone, and Slash inhales sharply. Something is off with her scent—he can't place it. He takes in the survivors, and his eyes come to rest on Jason, who was formally feral. He frowns.

Finally, his attention shifts to Scott as he scoops his sister into a tight embrace. Slash smells healing injuries. But they're faded, scenting of old wounds, though Slash knows they're not. A Combatant can heal almost as quickly as a Were. *Good thing for him.*

As if Scott intuits Slash's thoughts, Scott gives a chin lift over Jen's shoulder, meeting Slash's eyes. He bares his teeth slightly, sucking in a few quick chuffs. He scents something that makes his eyes snap to Julia.

Their scents have mingled—Scott and Julia's.

Slash's chin lowers, and he breaks eye contact, exhaling in frustration. This will complicate things. And he knows just the person to discuss it with. The others probably haven't scented anything yet. As a pureblood Red, Slash's scenting abilities far surpass anyone's.

Julia and Scott will already be aware of what's happened. Whether they've told anyone outside of their pairing, Slash doesn't know. He glances at Jason again, and the tight set of his jaw and his standoffish posture tells Slash that Jason suspects something is brewing.

"What is it?" Adrianna asks, searching his face, following his gaze like a tennis match gone wrong.

He cracks a smile.

"Besides the obvious?"

One side of her mouth lifts, and he's reminded of why he loves her. She's not classically beautiful, more like a pixie—cute and feisty. Still, she's the female for him. Blood calls to blood. There's no denying the primal absolutism of blood.

"Yeah," she replies softly. "You're looking awfully down for a buttload of Singers to have been found. I mean, this is great news. A Combatant is alive. Scott's brother and sister…"

"Michael's an asshole," Slash says without rancor.

"True." She smirks. "But we need all the color we can get right now. He's a smart ass, and he's obsessed with candy, but there's worse things." She shrugs.

Julia disengages from the little circle of rejoicing Singers and slowly walks toward Slash.

"Hey," she says with a smile.

Do you know your soul-meld is back online?

"Hi," he replies.

Adrianna looks between the two of them. "Got some serious shit to sling? Okay, I know when I'm not wanted."

"Adrianna—" Slash begins.

She twirls around, grabbing his hand. "It's cool, stud. Chill. I'll make myself busy."

That's what I'm afraid of.

Julia watches his eyes on Adrianna as she walks off. "She'll be fine, ya know."

He nods. But because he's an Alpha Red male, his instinct isn't a light switch to flick on and off. He *will* worry. When Adrianna is not in his presence, she will be on his mind.

Slash gives a rueful smile. "The wolf in me can't accept that."

Julia nods, frowning.

"What's on your mind?"

"Scenting," she replies immediately.

Slash's eyebrow jerks up. "For what?"

He smells her nervousness like a faint perfume in the air. He wonders if Julia knows his suspicions or if she's come to him for something entirely different.

"I—I need to know who is actually dead. A head count of sorts."

"I see."

Julia's face becomes apologetic. "I know it's a gruesome request…"

"Yes." It's the truth, and Slash won't sugarcoat it.

Julia's face falls.

"But I'm the Were for the job." His eyes scan the grounds, instinctively looking for Truman. He finds him hanging around with the sharp-tongued Singer-Were, Cynthia.

"Truman would be an excellent choice—or Zeke. Between the two or three of us, I think we can account for the casualties."

"I need to *know*, for closure," Julia explains in a voice ground down by tears and heartache.

"I understand." His face smoothes as he changes the subject. "Good news about the Singers."

She nods, and a soft sigh escapes. "It is, but—" She runs a hand over hair that's still damp from a shower. "I don't want any more surprises." Her luminous, cat-like eyes lock with his.

Slash folds his arms and dips his chin with acquiesce. "If there are supernaturals to find or save—ones who may still be living? We'll find them."

Another relieved breath leaks out of her. "Thank you, Slash."

"Welcome."

His eyes narrow on her. Anxiety fills his nostrils. "I know," he admits quietly.

Sudden color splashes against the pale skin of her face. "Oh."

Julia's head lowers, and long, champagne-colored hair swings forward, obscuring her expression.

"When will you tell him?" Slash asks.

She glances at him. "Pretty soon. He'll eventually scent the change anyway," she mutters.

Slash tenses. Serving up raw truth always feels wrong, but he doesn't know another way. "That's not what I'm asking."

Her chin jerks up, eyes fierce. "Do you think I like this back-and-forth shit? I hate it." Her voice hits the last word like a punch to the gut. "But there's nothing I can do. Tharell told us that the magic of faerie negated the soul-meld."

"Tharell's a liar, fey or not," Slash grinds out, still pissed the Sidhe was allowed to live. *Better to lop off his head and burn his ass to ashes.*

Julia meets his eyes. "The fey don't lie."

Slash jerks his head back at those words and the silence stretches between them.

"So you think he told you what was true for that time?"

Julia nods. "Exactly. By the time faerie's proximity was less, so was its hold on our bond. Then Scott was taken. We never found out until now."

Julia grapples with her emotions like a wrestler losing on the mat.

Finally, she appears to win the momentary struggle with her feelings. "And when Scott came back, I believed I was just glad to see him. Y know—relieved." She twists her hands.

Slash's lips lift, painfully pulling the pucker of scar tissue in his cupid's bow. "But you were *too* relieved."

Julia bites her lower lip and nods. "It's terrible. I'm the worst person on the planet."

Slash doesn't comfort others. He receives no comfort, either. He tries something new. "Maybe not the *very* worst."

Julia laughs. "Gee, thanks. You're a real prince."

Slash frowns. "I was trying to offer a little…"

"Salt in the wound?" She laughs, and it sounds like despair making a run for it.

"No," he says gravely. "I don't take pleasure in your pain. For someone so young, you have a lot on your shoulders."

Slash steps closer, putting a light hand on her upper arm, in defiance of his earlier sentiment. "Listen to me. These huge responsibilities won't lessen. They'll grow more complex, bigger. Take a mate." His eyes implore her to see reason. "Drop this human attitude and culture. It doesn't apply to us. You need a mate to help you carry these things that need attention."

"I can't choose between them, Slash." Her eyes meet his, and he's momentarily startled by the swimming bourbon irises. "I can't believe I'm blabbing all this stuff to you." She heaves a little self-conscious laugh.

Slash shrugs. "I scented it. There's no denying"—he taps the side of his beak—"the discernment. Besides, I'm not a chatty guy."

Julia breaks into a grin. "That, I know."

"Good."

They stare at each other for a handful of seconds. "I'll let you know. I have my own reasons to want to know who lives."

Julia's eyebrows pop. "Can I know what those are?"

He deliberates, unsure about whether to confide.

Slash is not an easy male.

He looks at Julia. Yet, she is not an easy female.

They make quite a pair.

"If Adrianna's packmaster is dead, she is free to mate with me."

"Wow," Julia says softly, seemingly stunned.

Slash feels his face heat. He understands her surprise, of course. That one as ugly as he would even imagine a life with a female like Adrianna is foolish.

But love is foolish. Love knows no bounds or reason. Love simply *is*. It grows from the fertile garden of the heart like a stubborn flower, to be adored by the recipient or rejected so the blooms can wilt in the shade of unrequited love.

He casts his eyes to the ground. "I don't deserve her." His voice is gruff, and Slash hears the shrug of dismissal in his own words.

"No, Slash. That's not it," Julia says, lightly touching his arm.

He looks up, seeing the compassion in her face, and looks swiftly away.

Slash doesn't need anybody's fucking pity. "I *understand* how I look. I get that I'm not a prize to be won."

"Hey," Julia says in a sharp voice, and he reluctantly turns to face her again. "Scars do not define the man, Slash."

He heaves a painful breath, jerking it from air that's grown thick with his regret about confessing to anyone. He should have kept his own council.

"She's from another pack. The home den mates with their own females," he explains.

"Pfft," Julia says with obvious disdain. "That's dumb."

Slash smiles blandly. "It is what it has always been."

"Well, if Lawrence isn't here to lay down the letter of the law, who's to stop you from marrying Adi?"

"Mating," he corrects.

"Right," she says with a smile.

Slash taps his temple. "You're still very human in your thought process."

"Maybe, but all that stuff is on my mind at the moment."

He nods. "No one is here to stop us. That's exactly my motivation for seeing it through. Though I would have done it for the asking."

Julia squeezes his forearm. "I know it. And I know Karl will help. He was a cop, after all."

Julia steps closer, and he looks down into her face—a face without guile. It makes him anxious to see someone so fragile lead so many.

"Does Adi know how you feel?"

His eyes don't flinch under Julia's intense scrutiny.

"Unfortunately, yes."

"Why, 'unfortunately'?"

Slash drags a hand over his short hair as he gives a harsh exhale, and Julia steps back, sensing the space he needs.

"She could do better. I am selfish in my pursuit."

"You're honest. And that's what Adi needs. You forget, I lived in that den for a while, and they were letting Tony rule the roost. Jason was locked up like an animal. If it hadn't been for Manny, I don't know what would have happened. Lawrence, in my opinion, was a weak leader, letting the Were kill each other for their stupid rites and treating the females like a commodity. I wasn't a fan."

Slash is troubled but not surprised. There simply aren't enough females. It's a cross-species dilemma. Slash has often wondered if the dwindling number of females is a type of natural selection in the supernatural realm. Nature does population control while affording extra protection for the females by making sure there were more than enough males to provide that protection. But it leads to corruption within the Were leadership.

"If Lawrence is gone, there will be no opposition. If he is not, I will appeal for the right to mate with Adrianna. In the meantime, Truman, Zeke and I will scent the deceased. I don't know everyone's unique scent, but I can identify the Were and give a count of how many Singers—"

Julia holds up her hand. "Thank you. Please, don't tell anyone what I've asked you to do. It's a grisly task, and emotions are already running high. People are just waiting for something else to wail and gnash. And"—Julia's eyes fill with tears—"I don't blame them one little bit."

Salt permeates the air, and Slash speaks to a point above her shoulder. "There is good in all of it. More Singers are alive. Tessa and Tahlia are solid additions."

Julia's brows furrow. "Yeah. What's their story?" She wipes tears from her face.

Slash throws a hard glance her way, his hands going to his hips.

"Whoa—that bad?"

Slash shakes his head. "No. It's not bad, but it's not perfect, either. The whelp—"

"Tahlia? Is she really a whelp?"

Slash's mouth twists into a smile. "No. But she is hardly more than one. She is Lanarre."

Julia's looks surprised. "I remember what that is. When I was bored out of my mind and semi-prisoner at the Northwestern pack, I read the Lycan history." Her frown turns to a confused scowl. "But a female Lanarre running around without guardians? From what I can recall, they are not unguarded until mated."

"Her guardians were murdered."

Her scowl deepens. "By who?"

"Who do you think?" Slash asks.

Julia shrugs, her expression puzzled. "I have no idea."

"Tony."

"Oh crap." Julia shudders. "What an evil guy he was."

"Yes."

Julia cups her elbows. "So, we're taking care of Tahlia until the Lanarre find us and kick our asses for having her?"

Slash barks out a laugh. "Pretty much."

"Great."

"It gets better."

Julia groans, and he's sympathetic.

"She was traveling to mate with her chosen."

Horror bleeds over Julia's face, her eyes widening. "Oh, wow."

Slash nods. "Basically, he's the prince of another Lanarre pack."

Julia's arms fall by her sides, palms out. "Does she want to marry this guy?"

"Don't you have enough politics to worry about?" Slash asks.

"Are you teasing me?"

Slash nods, allowing a smile to touch his lips. "A little."

"Hell, yes, I have enough. But, I don't want to just deliver Tahlia to this arranged-marriage dude—"

"Drek."

"Okay, *Drek.* No, I want to her to be willing."

Neither one talk about the parallels to Julia's own circumstances. They don't need to.

"Not our business. It's a Lanarre issue."

Her face puckers with distaste. "Uh-huh."

They're quiet for a time while Slash thinks. The Singers have moved inside the house to presumably eat and catch up more. Slash feels eyes on them, nonetheless.

He's sure Scott would not be out of eyesight, but within earshot. He doesn't scent Jason.

"And Tessa?" Julia inquires suddenly.

"She's on the run from the Western pack. Tramack."

"Weird name," Julia says. "Why is he after her?"

"Old-school pack." Slash knows of the Western. They border the Northwestern's territory, though they don't co-exist well.

Julia's eyebrow lifts and she tucks a loose strand of hair behind her ear. "What, like the Northwestern?"

Slash shakes his head. "No. They hold to very old principles that are dangerously outdated. But again, it's not our pack. I don't have jurisdiction there. Tessa says she's been running for twenty years." Slash gives her a sidelong glance. "There's a lot of dead Were in her wake."

Julia pulls a face, giving a surprised jerk of her chin. "Really?"

"Yes. She's learned to survive and the males aren't allowed to use deadly force. Tramack wants her for himself."

Disgust replaces surprise. "What a mess."

I agree. "She'll be here temporarily then she'll have to move on."

"Why doesn't this dweeb give up?"

Why indeed? Slash laughs abruptly then cuts it off. It's too somber tonight when he's on the brink of searching out death scents. His smile vanishes.

"Some Were become obsessed with a certain female, usually an Alpha. They can't think of anyone else. And, remember, there isn't a plethora of females."

"True, but who wants someone that doesn't want *them*?" Julia asks.

Slash gives a hard smile. "Plenty."

He allows his expression to convey that she should have known the answer to that question.

Her face tightens when understanding dawns.

"Right."

Neither mention Tony.

"I'll find the dead," Slash says, ending the conversation.

Julia nods sadly, giving him her back as she walks away.

Praile

"*D*o it."

Lazarus lays his palms on Praile's ruined shirt. He hisses from the light contact.

"The Master has commanded a three-quarter healing," Lazarus reminds him.

"I will deal with the Master. I cannot feign being a recovered Singer without this, Lazarus."

Seconds tick by, and Praile groans when the power of Lazarus's healing washes through the rough cotton, seeping into the rawest part of the torn flesh.

Vapor rises as the bloom of health surfaces to the newly healed skin.

Praile's head sinks forward, and he groans with relief, shuddering as the worst of the torment falls away.

Lazarus's hands lift, and Praile steps away, jerking the shirt from his skin.

It's the equivalent of ripping off a Band-Aid. Fresh scabs come away with the material, and he howls.

"Praile," Lazarus begins to reprimand, and Praile turns again.

They repeat a short bout of healing, and finally, Praile steps away the second time. His eyes search the woods, commanding the minions.

They slither out of the forest, tails high, horns long, their skin so dark it is black shadowed by red.

"Clothes," Praile instructs with a bark.

Lazarus quietly observes Praile making his way stiffly inside a new shirt. The waistband of the denims are drenched in his blood, and those must be replaced as well.

"Make haste. The perimeter is guarded."

Praile rolls his eyes. "I know that. We must make the most of this charade. The pretense will only need to be maintained for a day, perhaps a few hours more. We move in, kill the High One, and steal the blood babe and its mother from under their grieving noses. It's glaringly simple, Lazarus."

Doubt lingers at the edges of Lazarus's altered face. "I don't have time to convince you."

"You are here to scent track every supernatural in the area. I want Tharell if he's still alive."

"He is."

"The Master will take great pleasure in a promise broken by the Sidhe. Tharell can be fileted over and over and shall never die."

Lazarus's expression is carefully neutral, but Praile can see what swims beneath: loathing mixed with a glimmer of fear.

"It will keep the Master *very* occupied."

Lazarus raises a pale-blond eyebrow. "And his lashes off *your* skin."

Praile gives Lazarus a considering look. "Precisely."

Praile turns and commands the low demons telepathically. They retreat into the woods to blend with the organic matter until summoned once more. They're barely sentient, but they have their uses.

Grunts for his bidding. Demonic meat shields in battle.

The demonic low females have even more diverse uses. Praile licks his lips with his forked tongue in both memory and anticipation.

Soon. Soon he will leave this place and go back to his hot slice of dark heaven. There, he will feast at the Master's side once more, glowing in the adoration of a task well done. Tharell will be the literal whipping boy, the High One will be dead, and the last hope of the Singers will be snuffed out like a dying flame.

Praile cackles in joy. His deeds are nearly done.

He slips his cloak of false humanity over himself, rendering his skin, horns, and tail invisible. His tongue proves the most difficult. All his consonants come out with a hiss.

He is a handsome demon. Yet—all the attributes of his attractiveness are a challenge to hide. Nevertheless, Praile makes short work of cloaking his true being.

He will have to be constantly vigilant whenever he speaks. It wouldn't do to sound like a snake when he's remanded to Region One.

Just as he thought that, two Singer guards came upon him and Lazarus.

Fortuitous.

Praile and Lazarus raise their hands in an obvious gesture of truce.

The Singer at the left asks, "Who are you?"

"I'm Laz, from Region Two, and this is Peter"

Praile contains his irritation at being given the ill-suited name he did not agree to.

Good Lucifer.

The two Singers exchange a thoughtful glance. "How'd you get separated from Two?"

Lazarus smiles, and Praile bites his lip to keep from laughing. His mirth would certainly reveal their deception.

"We became separated during the battle and have just made our way here."

The Singers look suspicious, but the story agrees with everything they know thus far.

The Singer guards are not Angelic enough to have the veins that would alert them to the presence of cloaked demonics.

Fooling the High One will be a special bit of business.

The faster I end her, the better for us all.

"All right. We can use all the Singers we can get. You two follow us and shack up at Region One for the time being."

"Is the Rare One there?" Praile is dizzy with excitement about her impending death at his talons.

Mild puzzlement knots the Singer's brows. "Of course."

"Good." Praile nods, sensing Lazarus's discontent. "At least we have leadership after all the deaths."

The Singer's face smooths out, all suspicion gone. "Yes. It's the one positive in all the misery."

Praile gives a sad nod, as false as anything he's ever manifested.

They move ahead. He and Lazarus share a look of readiness behind their backs.

They're nearly there.

Tessa

Tessa feels like a million bucks. A hot shower and some food have made her wolf want to roll on its back and have its belly scratched. However, Tessa doesn't know anyone and decides it's better to take a walk down to the lake she spied earlier from a window instead of wallowing in her temporary reprieve.

Tessa feels night pushing at the edges of the day, pregnant with longing to birth the stars.

The moon beckons, just out of range, and Tessa sighs with longing. She can't count how many months have passed since she was able to just *be* her animal without fear of capture.

She has a chance to defend herself against males in her human form. But when in wolf form, the difference of genders is at its glaring fullest. In Tessa's opinion, the best advantage a female Were has going for her is the quarter-change. They look no different, but have heightened senses, strength, and speed. It's meant to be a protection against losing a whelp while pregnant, but the form can be conjured at will, without the moon.

She's never attacked Tramack's hounds while in human form. She met them all head on in her quarter-change form. They were at a disadvantage without their wolfen forms engaged.

And she brutally exploited it.

Tessa has no remorse. If Tramack allowed her freedom, she would no longer have to run. Sleeping in a different bed every two weeks, eat whatever she can forage—Tessa is merely existing. She simply takes sustenance, and breathing has begun to make her weary.

Pushing air in and out of her lungs is simply not enough in this life. Her will to live is slipping as Tramack gains ground in his chase. But as the moon begins to peek through clouds stretched thin like milky wounds, Tessa is happy for this moment. She is protected, and she has a full belly and a lighter heart than she's had in a years.

She's not a great musician, but she begins to whistle a melody—a tune she remembers from when she was a whelp.

Her mother and father raised her from whelphood before they were killed in one of the tragic wars of her kind. Being an orphan is not unique to the Were.

Maybe Were would be more fruitful if we stopped killing each other. Tessa thinks women could stop the wars if they were allowed to hold leadership roles.

The thing is, there simply aren't enough females to fulfill all the positions they should. Females are so scarce there's nothing soft to balance the hard. It's all raging testosterone. Battle, then sex, eat—rinse and repeat.

I know there's more.

A bird lands on a branch not too far away and twitters a last song. He stays long enough to offer solace then leaps off the branch to roost just as true night lands with a soft sigh all around her.

Tessa shivers inside the cooler nocturnal embrace, moving smoothly into quarter-change. Instantly, her higher body temperature warms her, and she rolls her shoulders back with an exhale of relief, comfortable again.

Her ears prick at the sound of approaching footsteps. She moves behind a tree that feeds directly from a lake, which is little more than a large pond. The water is beautiful, but the smells of death strangely linger. Her nose twitches with it.

Weird.

Tessa sights four figures walking toward her position and moves deeper into the shadows.

In this form, her eyes function as though it's daytime, and she's grateful anew for the blessings of the quarter-change.

Two Singer guards, whose names she doesn't know, move with purposeful strides toward the Singers' large mansion. It looms at the top of a small hill, and Tessa watches lights pop on inside like many eyes, casting false warmth against the grounds.

The two men walking behind the Singers catch Tessa's interest.

They move stiffly as though unaccustomed to their own gait, especially the bizarre-looking one to the right. Tessa flares her nostrils but doesn't catch a scent. The man is like a vampire, who doesn't carry a scent. Though sometimes, vamps do smell vaguely like earth and snakes. Tessa frowns.

The one to the left is tall. His pale hair is some shade of blond in daylight, but in the moonlight, it is silver.

His gaze flashes in her direction. His eyes are also light. Tessa's heart thuds. *He can't see me.*

Maybe he's a Tracker? Tessa doesn't enjoy being nose-blind. No Were does.

Clearly he doesn't belong here, and neither does she.

So they're equal. Tessa decides not to worry about it for now.

Something snaps behind her, and she whirls, talons spiking out of her fingertips in a painful burst. She's still in quarter by a thread. Tessa doesn't make a sound, planting her feet wide and crouching.

Then she recognizes Tahlia.

Tessa's embarrassed. She made a novice mistake by becoming so engrossed that she forgot her surroundings.

"You're defending yourself against me?" Tahlia asks in disbelief.

Tessa straightens, feeling a new flush of stupid. "No." Her talons slide back, and the fine hairs at her nape smooth against her sensitive skin. "I didn't scent you."

"Sloppy," Tahlia remarks with a little smile.

Tessa scowls.

"Thanks for nothing."

"Don't be cross. I think it's odd you missed me, is all." She hikes an inky eyebrow.

"Yeah. I was concentrating on them." Tessa points to the four males who are almost to the front porch of the mansion.

She twists in their direction, her eyes narrowing at the men. "Hmm. Who are they?"

"Don't know."

"You don't sound as though you're too thrilled."

"Nope. Don't like it."

Tahlia turns back, her eyes are navy pools of midnight. "Why?"

Tessa blows out a frustrated breath. "Listen, you seem like a nice kid. But it's only a matter of time until Drek finds you and it's faerie tale time."

Tahlia blinks.

"For me?" Tessa plants her thumb between her breasts. "I have to consider *everyone* to be a threat. And it's just a little bit *too* convenient those two show up right after us, from the same direction we came from. Nah, I don't like it on principle. Plus, I can't scent them."

Tahlia's quiet.

Finally, Tessa says, "Well?"

Tahlia gives her a sidelong glance, her lips pulling into a small smile. "I think we should find out who they are. I have to keep busy with something."

Tessa lets out a breath, feeling as though she just passed a test. "Thanks."

Tahlia shrugs. "For what?"

"For being my only friend."

Tahlia's smile widens and she lifts a delicate shoulder. "You're my only friend too."

Tessa's grin slips. "Why? Didn't you have some whelplings to hang out with among the Lanarre?"

"Common Were? Certainly." Tahlia's smile is a flat line. "Now ask me if I was allowed to belong? To be a part of anything?"

"Were you?"

Her voice goes low as she answers, "No. Never."

"Why the hell not?" Tessa shakes her head in mild disgust. "Y'know, for being *it* for Lycan kind, being Lanarre sounds pretty sucky."

"It wasn't my role."

Tessa gives her a sharp look. "What is then?"

Tahlia eyes fall away from Tahlia's to train on the perfect half-moon. "Whatever they have of me."

Julia

Though Julia's circle of trustworthy supernaturals grows, it's still small.

Scott and Jason stand at her side while she tries not to let the strengthening soul-meld out of the bag like an escaped cat.

Tharell needs to be questioned.

The scar at his throat pulses like a lavender creek that runs with thin blood beneath it. Julia's own throat tightens at the sight, and she couldn't swallow if her life depended on it.

Scott takes her hand, and the knot in her chest loosens. She can breathe—and think. And she'll need to because Tharell holds answers to important questions. His knowledge is one of the key reasons she didn't have him killed as so many wanted.

She hides her gratefulness for Scott's gesture, and he squeezes her hand when he feels it course through him. Their bond makes secrets impossible. It's a relief, and a curse, to have it back.

Jason stiffens and Tharell smiles from his bound position at the ground.

"Trouble in paradise?" he murmurs, his beautiful turquoise eyes bright, though hardly any light reaches the deepest part of the Singer training barn.

A small window, too tiny to fit anyone older than a nine year old through, allows pale moonlight to slant inside. The illumination strikes Tharell's deep-purple hair, turning it into a spoiled-plum color.

Julia doesn't bother with fabrication. "Yes."

She grabs Jason's other hand, and he looks down at her, his eyes shadowed.

"I already know, Jules."

She bows her head, and Tharell laughs. Welling despair rises inside Julia like a geyser, threatening to burst from her mouth and force her to verbalize things she would rather not say.

Tharell quips. "So human—yet not."

"Shut the fuck up."

"Can't argue with that, Caldwell," Scott adds.

Tharell grins at their discontent, and Julia is plagued with second thoughts about letting him live and the shame of thinking it.

Jason tenses. "No—Scott, kicking his teeth in won't solve anything."

"But it'll make me feel so much better," he says.

Jason barks out a laugh. "Amen to that."

"You wouldn't be so sure of yourself if I was unbound and deep within the arms of the sithen. There, it is I who maintains all the power," Tharell says in a bald voice.

Jason shrugs his words away. "You're a dick."

Tharell turns his penetrating glare to Jason. "Your crude names do not move me, Singer."

"I can think of something that will," Scott says and steps forward.

Something painful flares inside Julia's gut, and she gasps.

Scott stops mid-stride, and he whips his head around to look at her. Jason's hand moves to her back. "What?" they ask at the same time.

The three of them look at Tharell.

His veins glitter black beneath his plum-colored skin, rising to the surface to pulse in time to his heartbeat.

Julia's mimic his, but hers are golden-silver and perfect, like jeweled lace.

Her belly begins to throb with the beginnings of something that pulls her toward Tharell. She takes a single, staggering step toward him.

"Ahh…" he says, relaxing against his binds.

"What. The. Fuck?" Jason yells, dropping her hand and going for Tharell.

Scott grabs his arm.

Jason whirls, narrowly missing Julia as his fist reactively plows toward Scott's jaw.

Scott jerks his face away, narrowly missing the blow intended for Tharell.

Tharell chuckles as Julia drops to her knees, cradling her stomach with both arms.

"What have you done?" she whispers. Scott and Jason turn, their hands fisted in each other's shirts.

"It is not I who has done anything. But the saber."

Julia forgets that her soul-meld with Scott is suffocating them, falling back two-fold as it pours into the crevices as though it never left.

She doesn't recall that her husband is ready to come to blows with Scott again or that Tharell should never see her bare skin.

Julia rips off her shirt. Scattered buttons fly like plastic raindrops. She throws the long-sleeved shirt to the bare cement floor.

She tears her cami sky high, looking down at the horror on her stomach.

Scott falls beside her, his large palm covering where the saber struck and Cyn healed her.

His eyes bulge. "Ah!" he says in a hoarse shout.

But his palm can't hide the damage. A comma-shaped whip of black stands above her belly button. Where she was pierced with the blade, spiderweb-fine threads spread from the deep blackness, lined in red.

This morning, the mark appeared to be a bruise. It pulsed and itched, and Julia had assumed the sensation represented residual healing. Too many things clamored for her attention for her to worry about a healing wound.

But this wound isn't healing. It's spreading like a contagion.

The finer ends of the ebony threads extend to her ribcage.

"You sicken," Tharell says with utter certainty, eyes on the spreading black highway of encroaching marks. His eyes alight on Scott's face like blue fire. "She slows its progress but not the inevitable."

"Why?" Julia cries.

"The blood of the demonic has entered your system. Even as the Blooded Queen and your precious angelic blood combat the spore—it is insufficient protection."

Scott lets go of Julia's skin as if it burns him, and he grabs Tharell off the floor, hiking him until their noses meet.

He shakes Tharell. "Tell me how to undo this?"

"No," Tharell says with a cunning smile.

Scott drops him with a grunt of disgust, and Tharell stands, though his feet and hands are bound.

Scott retreats one step and clocks Tharell in the face.

The blow rocks the Sidhe warrior back against the wall, and he spits black blood onto the concrete between them. "Strike me all you wish, but it will not save her life."

"What will?" Jason asks.

Julia lifts her head at the sound in his voice—inescapable consequence.

Julia totally knows the answer.

"Give her up, Were."

Jason whirls, beating the wall with bruising force. "No!" he bellows.

Julia covers her ears.

Hot tears roll down her cheeks and splash at her knees, dampening her jeans like drops of sorrow in a sea of denim.

Her heart thumps against her calm, eating at it with each beat. Resignation crushes her spirit.

"This isn't what I planned, Caldwell," Scott says. "I'd never cause her this kind of sorrow if I had a choice."

On her knees, Julia looks up at Scott.

Jason turns, fists at his side, veins standing out like stark pathways of rage on his flesh.

Julia quickly gets to her feet, standing between them.

Tharell remains silent against the wall. His swollen lip heals as he watches the emotional war between the three of them.

"Julia," Scott says in a low voice, gently moving her so that she is no longer between him and Jason, setting her farther away from Tharell. The growing evil in her belly quiets at Scott's touch.

"I feel it," he says quietly.

"I know." Julia can't keep the relief out of her voice when the seed of evil flinches from her soulmate's touch.

"Stop talking in fucking code," Jason yells at them and Julia flinches. Spittle stands at the corner of his mouth.

As Julia gazes at Jason, she realizes for the first time that maybe, what's happened to both of them separately in the last three years, might make it impossible for them to be together now, with or without the soul-meld. What Julia needs is to take care of her people, not walk on eggshells around Jason.

She needs someone who thinks of others first and doesn't react with anger whenever something doesn't go his way. Those revelations move through her mind like a flash flood.

Jason sees them anyway.

"What? Is this it, Jules? You get a little soul juice back, and it's all about Scott again?"

Julia's silent. Finally she shakes her head. "I don't feel like having this discussion in front of Tharell."

"Do not mind me," Tharell says unhelpfully.

"Shut up." Jason shoots him a hard look, and Tharell smirks, shrugging.

Jason turns back to Julia and she sighs. "I am sick. There might not be any *me* to have." Julia's eyes search his wild ones. "You're so caught up on having me like a favorite bone you can't see the bigger picture."

He folds his arms. "Nope. Don't see it."

Where has Jason gone? More than that—*why haven't I noticed?*

Maybe she hadn't wanted to. "Tharell's awful, but he's right. There was demon's blood…"

"A high demon. The lowly would not have adequate power to sicken the Blooded Queen."

"What?" Julia asks.

Tharell hops a step away from the wall, and Scott moves protectively in front of Julia. She grasps his biceps, feeling the hard muscle beneath.

"Say what you have to say from there, asshole," Scott says.

"There are high demons. I have demonic blood, as we've already determined. The high demon in charge of these matters is called Praile. He is who would have instructed Tony to slaughter the Singers of this region, weakening them so the Blooded Queen might be unguarded. It was a stroke of luck for the demonic that Julia was pierced with the saber."

"No Combatant to help her," Scott says thoughtfully.

Tharell shakes his head. "I was called upon when the lowly appeared for battle. I partook because I had no choice."

Tharell lifts his healed chin, his disdain clear. "Blood rules all."

Julia believed it. If she'd learned nothing else within the last three years, it was that.

Blood governs us all.

"So I die?" Julia whispers, fighting tears. *After coming all this way, some demonic blood is going to kill me.* She's been poisoned, hunted, kidnapped, and stabbed. *But this?*

She has people to rule, things that matter beyond her own self.

For the moment, she will have to ignore the underlying tension between Jason and her. The Singers come first. But she can't rule if she dies.

Then Tharell surprises her. "No. You will not die from this alone. But a high demon can finish the job."

"Fat chance." Jason gestures around him. "We've got plenty enough guys sitting around, waiting for the chance to kick some demon ass. The fire dicks missed their window. Too bad, so sad. "

Tharell inclines his head. "No one would be a proper match for the likes of Praile."

Jason's jaw works back and forth. "Some kind of fire prick struts in and kills Julia?"

"He will be able to sense our blood within her body."

"So we're screwed?" Jason presses.

"What? Is *he* our advisor now?" Scott stares at Jason, palm flung toward Tharell. "This fey is the one who betrayed us, tried to kill another Sidhe warrior, and we've kept alive only for answers I'm not even sure we want or should listen to."

"Kill me and take away more answers," Tharell comments in a sage voice.

Julia asks, "Why, Tharell? Why would you do this?"

Tharell's face shuts down. "You are a true and honest leader, Julia. However, in faerie, I am merely tolerated because my blood is not pure. When Queen Darcel was murdered by the lovely Delilah, I was free of some of it. But I will never be released from the prejudice of the pureblood Unseelie in a place where I must dwell to flourish. Further, my actions are moderated by my mixed genetics—I must do exactly as I am told. And"—his eyes sink into hers like barbs—"no one has asked the right question."

Julia moves toward him, and Scott tries to stop her.

"No, Scott—"

Tharell's so tall, she cranes her neck to meet his eyes. Her mind turns over the facts of how Tharell has behaved. Suddenly, she hits on the reason. The answer was in Jacqueline from the beginning.

"If you were to never leave faerie—the sithen—would you be okay?"

Tharell smiles. "That, my Blooded Queen, is the right question."

Their gazes lock as though no one else exists. Right now—for Julia, no one does. The world consists of only her and Tharell.

"What's the answer?" Julia keeps her eyes on his face as if it's a target. Before he replies, his expression gives away the answer—and something else.

Relief.

"Yes," he answers.

She can see that he's relieved that someone could look beyond his deeds. Jacqueline isn't the only one who's crazy outside of faerie.

For some, insanity is the gift of leaving the sithen.

For Tharell, with his demonic blood, it was a death sentence.

But Julia's willing to offer a stay of execution—if she lives long enough.

Julia is glad when they leave Tharell in his cell. The two men wish for his death while Julia longs for less suffering.

She strides toward the one person she knows is insurance against Tharell. She needs to get him to faerie, but she can't have him doing more things against her while he's under the influence of demonic intent and insane due to his distance from faerie.

The only one who's a threat to him will be his guard, if she's willing. Julia hopes for Tharell's sake that she is.

Julia's nearly at a jog, but Jason and Scott are walking fast, easily keeping up to her five feet four inches.

"We haven't figured anything out, Jules."

Julia whirls on him, jabbing her finger into his chest. "My life is a mess. I'm sorry. But I didn't ask to be taken back in Alaska any more than you asked to be attacked and turned." Her eyes blaze into his, and Jason doesn't drop her stare.

"Why is the answer to saving you always me letting you go?" he asks softly. His response deflates her anger.

Julia's finger drops as her top lip rolls between her teeth. Seconds later, she replies, "I don't know."

She stares at him, looking over a man who, by human standards, she's married to. He's handsome, protective, and smart. They have a long history together. They've been through so much—too much.

Her heart feels like it's in her throat, and Julia stifles a sob when she realizes she's fallen out of love with Jason.

She tries to rationalize her feelings. *Maybe it's the soul-meld.*

But maybe it's just life, the life she did not choose.

"I can smell it on you, Jules."

She startles as though she spoke her horrible epiphany aloud. But she didn't.

"What?" she asks softly.

Jason flicks a glance at Scott, who's stood by her side silently for the entire thing.

Scott steps toward Jason. "Fuck you, Caldwell."

Julia wants to scream at them and beat on their chests. But they're doing such a great job of it without her.

Jason heaves a sigh of utter disgust. "Take off. Give us a minute. I'm not going to hurt Julia."

Scott folds his arms across his muscular chest. "You don't have a great track record, Jason."

He nods. "I know, but I have a handle on my shit. Just—*God*, do you have an ounce of compassion?"

Scott stands there for a moment then gathers Julia against him. He kisses the top of her head and says softly, "I won't be far."

Julia nods and feels a sensation like physical tearing when he leaves. The demon's blood pulses back to sick life with each step he takes away from her. Julia folds her arm over her stomach and reluctantly turns to Jason.

He plows his fingers through his longish hair, and Julia notices it needs a trim. "I can smell *him*."

"I didn't know."

"I know. It's *never* your fault." He gives a little crazy nod. "But this time, I can't do it. To save your life, I could pull through like I was going to before."

With William, she thinks but doesn't say.

"But I can't stand by and watch some other guy have you. It's not right."

"Are you standing by us being married?"

He shakes his head, and Julia can see his sadness even in the weak artificial light cast between the barn and the mansion.

"Nah. I know none of that matters a damn to these people." He laughs, swinging out a palm. "That's right—we're not really human anymore. All the stuff of our past, the shit that mattered? Gone." He throws his arms up into the sky, beseeching a break that'll never come.

Julia doesn't say anything, because he's right. Their past is just that—the past.

"So, I'm going to stick around until we know you're okay. Then I'm outta here."

Julia steps forward. Jason retreats a step, hands up in mock surrender. "Don't touch me, Jules. I can only take so much."

She stops. Her belly hurt, but her heart hurts more.

Julia doesn't allow more tears to fall, but she feels sick as she watches Jason walk down to the lake and away from her.

Julia

*J*ulia grows chilled as the night deepens. Long after his broad back disappears from view, her eyes remain on the empty spot where Jason disappeared by the lake.

Julia feels him before Scott moves behind her and wraps his strong arms around her. The top of Julia's head tucks easily beneath his chin, and Scott lays the side of his face against her hair.

"I can't say I'm sorry, and for that, I'm sorry."

Julia nods at his contrary statement because speaking is too difficult. The demon's blood growing inside her recoils inside her body at his nearness, and she feels momentary relief from its insidious progress as it grows sluggish.

"That's not really an apology, ya know," Julia manages to whisper.

"I know. I'm a real ass. But you're aware."

"Yes," she says, mad at him though she's a part of him now—again.

Scott turns her to face him. "Listen to me." His eyes seem to search every pore of her face and finally settle back on her gaze. "It's like I told Caldwell—if I had a choice, I'd allow you to be happy. I can't stand the idea of your sadness."

"Especially now," Julia says.

He grips her upper arms, pulling her tightly against his chest and cupping the back of her head. "Especially now."

Their foreheads touch, and his scent overwhelms her, engulfing her senses.

Julia swims through the headiness of his nearness enough to say, "I need to talk to someone. She can be a guard for Tharell. Get him back to faerie before something else happens and we're forced to kill him."

Scott pulls away, staring at her. "Killing Tharell would be awesome, Julia."

She gives a tight shake of her head, whipping her long hair back and forth. "Not for me."

Scott studies her then bends over. He kisses her forehead then moves to her eyelids. Her breaths begin to come deep and even. She feels as though she's always been in his arms.

"You're soft in all the places that matter," he whispers against her temple, "but I'm not."

Julia opens her eyes and his are liquid night. "I'm trying to look for something good here, Scott. Something that doesn't involve me hurting, killing or otherwise causing harm to someone else."

"We're good."

"Why?" Scott asks, squatting down to look into her eyes. He traps her face with his palms. "Why are you so afraid of the soul-meld?"

"Because it's wrecked Jason. And that's the last thing I'd never want to do, especially to him."

She wraps her arms around her torso, and Scott's palms slip from her face to thumb the back of her skull, stroking her neck. "He *knows*, babe. He knows you weren't trying to hurt him. He just can't let you off the hook." His hand flips open. "Jason's got to blame someone—and you're it."

"What do you mean you're hard and I'm soft?" Julia asks suddenly, ignoring his last comment.

Scott sighs, stepping away. He takes hold of her hand as his other drops from her nape. They begin walking toward the mansion.

Scott's lips quirk.

"Mind out of the gutter, Scott."

"You did say I was hard."

"You called me soft," she counters.

Scott gives her a speculative look. "True."

"I can't believe we're talking like this," Julia admits with a touch of shame.

"It's hard to keep up the pretense when we're connected like this. It's a tie at the molecular level. No one could resist it."

Julia stops.

"Wait."

Scott's dark eyebrow lifts.

"The soul-meld didn't reconnect until after…"

"I was tortured."

A lone tear slides out of her eye at the thought of anything hurting Scott.

Scott thumbs away the wetness. "Shh, babe, come here." He pulls her into his body, and Julia sobs. "I'm okay. I'm here—don't worry."

"What would I have done without you?" she whispers as she clutches at his shirt.

"What you've been doing."

Julia pulls away, her gaze riveted on his, debating about how much she should admit. "I wanted you when you were missing."

Scott's surprise is plain to see. "Without the meld?"

Julia nods. "Yeah," she whispers. "Yeah, I did."

Julia's face is wet with tears, but she makes no move to wipe it dry because Scott shocks her again.

"I realized when they were peeling my body apart—"

Julia covers her mouth and grabs his shirt, laying her face against his chest. His heart beats against her cheek, and an exhale shudders between them.

"I realized that I actually loved you, without the meld. Just me—Scott."

Julia nods against his chest. "But I love Jason, too."

Scott stills and takes her away from him.

"You love him?"

She nods.

Before he has a chance to react, Julia puts one hand on his shoulder, and the other on his face. "It's you who I'm *in love* with."

He grins. "Figured."

Julia snorts, a sad smile plucking the corners of her mouth and she pinches the cleft in his chin together. "Arrogant, more like."

"Yeah," he admits. His face sobers. "But my dad didn't die for nothing. I'm older, I'm Singer royalty. Our union makes sense in the cosmos."

Julia's smile twists. "You didn't think so when we first met."

He ducks his head. "A classic case of asshole-itis."

"Uh-huh."

Scott pecks her on the lips and with a little groan he whispers against the corner of her mouth, "Just so you know, I'm holding back. Giving you time."

To reconcile things with Jason. "I know."

Julia puts her hands on the hard planes of his chest and gives him a little shove.

He grabs her around the waist. "You're not getting rid of me that fast."

Julia wrinkles her nose and he kisses the tip.

"I need to see Delilah."

Scott jerks his chin back. "No shit?"

"Yes." She laughs. "She'll be Tharell's guard."

"My half-sister?"

"She's like Madonna." She disengages her arm and puts a hand on her hip. "Is there another Delilah?"

Scott releases her, acting as if he's thinking about it. Putting a finger to his chin, he rolls his eyes skyward.

"Knock it off." Julia smacks him on the arm and he picks her up in his arms again.

"Scott!" she laughs. "Can't—breathe!"

"Quiet," he says, pecking her on the lips again.

She looks up at him and his eyes are dark with something besides color.

Desire clouds them, vying for position in all that brown.

"Probably another Delilah somewhere in the world," he says in a voice choked by restrained emotion.

"Did someone call me?"

"Speak of the devil," Scott says in a dry voice. He carefully sets Julia on her feet.

Delilah looks between the two of them skeptically. "What's going on?"

"Soul-meld's back," Scott says without preamble.

Delilah's eyes widen ever so slightly. "Ouch—settle down, brother."

He scrubs his head. "It's been a long night."

Delilah's chin kicks up, and she saunters closer, looking them over so closely that Julia can feel the blood rush to her face.

"Waste of blood, that," Delilah comments, and Julia's hands automatically move to cover her cheeks.

Delilah giggles, and Scott moves between them.

"Don't worry, big brother. I don't like girls, though her blood *does* sing."

Julia's face snaps to Delilah's. She hasn't heard that expression since William said it. A stab of pain pierces her with the reminder. Her ultimate protector, William had nothing to gain from saving her life, but the love he held for her. It was a pure sacrifice, and she'll never forget it.

Delilah gives her a quizzical look. "Yes. Though I am meant to take a male's blood, yours does hold a…certain appeal."

"Keep the appeal to yourself," Scott says in warning that borders on a growl.

Silence sits heavy in the pause.

"Noted." Delilah answers then turns to Julia, clearly dismissing Scott. An inquisitive expression rides her face.

Now that Delilah stands before her, Julia's request seems like too much to ask.

Delilah studies her face. "Ask."

Julia sees the resemblance between her and Jacqueline, though she doesn't think mentioning it will ingratiate her to Delilah.

"I—can you escort Tharell to faerie?"

Delilah gives an abrupt laugh. "The murdering Sidhe?"

Julia instantly feels dumb for asking. Said like that, there is no way to deny that he's more than a murderer.

"Yes."

Delilah laces her fingers together in a gesture hauntingly like Jacqueline's. Scott's hand kneads her shoulder gently.

Julia gulps then pushes forward, "I don't *want* to kill him," she admits in a low voice. Though God knows, Tharell deserves it.

Delilah rolls her eyes, and Julia quickly continues, "And it has come to my attention that he went bonkers because he was outside the sithen and his demonic blood became dominant once he was far enough away from faerie to negate the effect of faerie's proximity."

"Ah," Delilah replies noncommittally. Her dark eyes, so similar to Scott's, sparkle like black diamonds. It's disconcerting how little Julia can read her expression.

"And I'm his natural enemy, so I will be able to keep him in line?" Coal-black eyebrows arch to her hairline.

Julia nods tentatively. "That's the idea."

Delilah's ebony gaze finds Julia again. "What does everyone else think?"

Julia bites her lip.

"Oh, this is funny. You've told no one?"

Julia shakes her head. *I knew it wouldn't be a popular idea.*

"She doesn't need to, Delilah. She's the Rare One."

"That's not it though, is it?" she asks softly, giving Julia an appraising look.

Julia shakes her head. "No. I don't have the energy to defend my theory to everyone who wants him dead. Not now. Not with everything that's changed recently."

"Ah. And Jacqueline—my mother—does she influence you in this?"

Delilah is no dummy. "Yes, in a way. I've seen the huge change since she spent time in faerie, and I have to assume—to believe—it could be true of Tharell."

Delilah's brow furrows as Julia hold her breath.

"Fine, I'll do it."

"She wasn't really asking," Scott says.

Julia lets tense breath out. "Shh, Scott." She puts a finger to his lips, and her eyes move to Delilah. "I would never issue an order. Tharell could harm you."

Delilah yawns.

"Not likely."

Huh. Julia doesn't know what to say to that. "Okay, what do you think?"

"I'll take the naughty Sidhe."

Thank God. Julia stretches out her hand, and Delilah takes hold of it, slowly shaking it to seal the deal. Julia pretends to ignore the hint of fang showing in her smug smile.

Her nostrils flare, and her fangs grow a touch longer. "My control is not limitless. Your blood is quite—" She stills, her hand clutching Julia's in a grip she could never break from. "Tasty." Delilah gives a nervous little lick of her lips.

"Back off, sis," Scott says. His words are light, but the meaning behind them is dead serious. Julia doesn't have to look at his face to know it. His feelings tear through the meld and hit her own.

"So yummy," Delilah says then appears to snap out of it, dropping Julia's hand and moving back a few steps out of the vague light between the two buildings. The shadows consume her form. "Where's Tharell?"

"I'll take you to his cell."

Scott, Julia and Delilah make the short trek to Tharell's cell.

Julia screams as Tharell comes into view, blood pouring out of his body.

Someone has executed vigilante justice.

Delilah blurs to his side, dropping beside him. A crimson pool leeches into the long skirt she wears, dying the gauzy fabric red. The small bells sewn into the fabric no longer ring as they clog with the Sidhe's blood.

Tharell turns his head. "Do not bother to heal me. It is a fatal blow."

Delilah gives an exasperated snort. "Nonsense, Sidhe. You've claimed immortality. Do not make yourself a liar."

"No," Scott says in a low voice.

"Yes," Julia returns like a volley.

Scott glowers at her, but Delilah turns her head away from them to look at Tharell as her delicate fangs slide out. "Trust me," she says awkwardly.

Julia should stop this, but she doesn't. She lets Delilah do what she does next.

Delilah tears open her own wrist.

"Drink from me, fey."

Tharell regards her.

Julia looks away from them as the noise of his suckling reaches her ears. Bright shame and memories well inside her. Images of William and her time in the coven are mixed with her relief to no longer be there. She comes back to the present with a start as Scott holds her while Tharell feeds from Scott's sister. It is one of the weirdest sights she's ever witnessed.

The blood flow slows from the gap in Tharell's body then stops.

Tharell sits up, unbound, and Delilah's wrist falls limply, her eyes at half-mast.

She's vulnerable. Tharell could kill her.

"Scott?" Julia's voice is full of fear.

But Tharell doesn't hurt Delilah. He gathers her against him. Her pale skin and dark hair look so beautiful against all his violet flesh.

When Tharell strikes her in the neck, Scott doesn't react at first.

But Delilah does.

Her head rolls away, and Tharell grunts, jerking her more tightly against his muscular body. His violet fingertips bit into ivory flesh.

What the fuck is happening? "Stop!" Julia shouts, adrenaline kicking her in the butt.

Then something wonderful happens. Tharell threads his fingers into the long strands of Delilah's hair, and his blue eyes regard Julia over Delilah's shoulder.

Sanity has returned and he is Tharell again—not the murderer, but the Sidhe warrior he was when she first met him.

He is also more than he seems, not just fey or demonic: *a vampire*, awoken by another right before their eyes.

Praile

*P*raile feels right at home, taking in the elegant head-quarters of his nemeses. Instinctively, he senses the lack of high Angelic blood quantum in the Singers present.

He and Lazarus will not be outed. The revelation relaxes him.

He frowns again. The single thing that *could* get their collective geese cooked would be the appearance of Region Two Singers who do not recognize them.

Ultimately, Praile and Lazarus are in a race against time to locate the High One and the one who carries the blood babe within her.

Lazarus gives him a full look of warning, and Praile scowls at him.

Praile does not need prompting from anyone, especially another high demon who is second to him. Praile functions with perfect autonomy.

The two Singer guards leave them inside an impressive foyer, with a mention that someone will be with them shortly.

Praile sighs with boredom, surveying the age of the structure. It is too modern for his taste, but he always liked the medieval times. Late nineteenth century is just not for him. *Too much artifice.* He's a sucker for the medieval torture racks—and the despair that permeated the air like a fragrance. *Now* that *was living.*

Praile hears footsteps approach then his blood rushes to the surface of his skin. Just when he believed he would get away with everything, an Angelic enters the foyer.

He is a handsome specimen. As Praile looks on with distaste, he must concentrate to keep the manifestation of his demonic blood from being obvious.

Praile is hanging on by a thread.

His pure demon blood is an oil-slicked cauldron boiling beneath his false human flesh. Lazarus copes better. However, Lazarus is a high demon, as well. Their blood is designed to serve as a natural alarm to their worst enemy's presence. The Angelic share that defense mechanism.

The effort of maintaining his camouflage makes sweat break out on Praile's skin, and his fingertips tingle as the large Singer approaches.

With each step the Singer takes, something primal and deep within Praile tightens. His teeth clench with the effort to retain his form.

"I am Victor," the Singer says. Eyes like pale gray storm clouds stare with disconcerting intensity on Praile. He is not intimidated by anyone.

Praile's situation is precarious.

He must persevere and use the speech that might be expected. "I'm Peter and this is Laz," Praile replies, swinging a casual thumb toward Lazarus.

Victor's perfect brow puckers. He looks from Praile to Lazarus. Praile's disquiet deepens. He feels strongly that it is critical this one must accepts them.

Kill him if he does not believe, he sends in telepathic command to Lazarus.

Praile does not want to show their hand at this juncture. However, they might not have a choice.

Yes.

"I do not know you," Victor says with quiet certainty.

For Satan's sake, he's Region Two.

Praile spreads his hands away from his body, cursing the horrible clothing. "We came as the battle commenced."

Understanding lights Victor's eyes. "Ah, I see." Victor knots his hands behind his back then glances at Praile. "I was not a part of the battle with the demonic." Praile gives a covert glance to Lazarus. "I was *here* when a Were went berserk and slaughtered Region One."

"How was it *you* endeavored to escape?" Lazarus asks.

Too formal, make your speech casual. Use slang, fool.

Lazarus flinches slightly from the mental plow Praile uses on his mind.

He is not subtle.

Victor's laser attention moves to Lazarus—through him. "There is a life bunker below the headquarters. All Regions have this safety contingency. I gathered whoever was royal, the females, children and secured them. We were automatically released earlier today."

Ah, makes perfect sense. Praile enjoys knowing the secrets of his enemies. Though before the High One came into being, it was of no purpose to pursue them in this way. The attempts of the demonic against the angelic would have been war without reason.

The Master is pragmatic, among other things.

Praile lifts his chin. "We survived the battle but were separated from the main group and made our way back here just now. We had only a vague idea of where Region One was located." He whips a casual palm around. "We're transplants," Praile embellishes.

Victor's eyes rest on his form. Praile notices Victor is not subtle, either, taking in Praile's stiff denims, shoes too bright a white, and ill-fitting shirt.

Praile sweats without his vapor to assist off-gassing his naturally searing skin. He uses every ounce of subversive magic to cause his clothes to appear as though they're worn, but he can only do so much. Splitting his concentration among the call of the blood, and his tail, his horns, and his skin color, he is leaking his effort everywhere.

He sees Lazarus tense nervously. Praile's machinations are obvious to him—but Praile doesn't know if they are as transparent to Victor.

Victor's face breaks into a smile. "Excellent. You are welcome here. We've lost so many of our kind it's a gift to find Singers who survived the siege."

Victor's skin glitters with blood reacting to the demonic within Praile and Lazarus.

However, he has not noticed. Lazarus's eyes widen as Victor claps Praile on the back, and he stumbles, forgetting the strength of a Singer with enough Angelic blood to be problematic.

Victor quirks a brow.

Praile raises his lips in the parody of a self-effacing smile, trying not to gaze at the Singer's veins. "I'm not known for my grace."

Victor shrugs. "That's fine. I don't know my own strength." He winks and begins to walk away, motioning for them to follow.

Praile wants to bash the Angelic's head in with his spiked tail.

A hand appears at his elbow.

Lazarus.

He gives the minutest shake of his head.

An exhale whistles out between Praile's teeth, regulating his anger. Strong emotion will make hanging onto his cloaking more difficult. Already he's lost enough control that the Singer's blood has risen to the top of his flesh.

How long will it be before he sees his own body's defenses and takes action?

Praile seethes and rails against the Singer who casually walks in front of them.

Victor enters a kitchen and spins around suddenly.

Praile smiles falsely.

Victor's words freeze on his tongue. "What is wrong with your mouth?"

Demon dammit. His teeth and tongue are exposed.

Lazarus moves quickly, bashing the Singer in the side of his neck with his forearm. He crumples.

"Come on, Praile," Lazarus urges.

Praile moves in quickly, grabs the Singer by the armpits, and drags him off. "Where did he say the bunker was?"

Victor's heels make black marks on the oak floors.

Praile rolls his eyes, looking around frantically.

Faint voices reach his ears.

"Lucifer help us," Lazarus bites.

"Think," Praile hisses, his forked tongue shredding the word.

Lazarus yanks the semi-conscious Singer toward the center of the hall, tearing an expensive oriental carpet from the middle and exposing a trapdoor.

Praile pops it open with a twist and a pull. A vacuum lock wheezes air.

They gaze down a dark hole with ladder-type steps.

A shuddering exhale blows out of Praile. Lazarus gives him a nod, and together, they roll the Singer toward the hatch then push him inside. The body of the unfortunate Angelic clunks down the short flight to land with a thud below.

Praile straightens, and Lazarus closes the circular portal. It makes a beeping sound and five shrill chimes, then a great suction sounds off for half a minute. All the while, they check that others don't wander in during the middle of their subterfuge.

No one does.

The portal locks, and a timer appears on its smooth surface. It's some kind of countdown clock.

Perfect.

It reads seventy-one hours and fifty-seven minutes. *Plenty of time.*

Praile is not humorless. After all, having a sense of humor is critical to surviving life in Hades and surviving the Master.

He grins. "One Angelic down."

"The rest to follow," Lazarus finishes grimly.

"Lighten up, Lazarus."

Lazarus cocks an eyebrow at the foreign expression. "I don't think this is a 'light' mission, Praile."

Praile glances down at the carpet covering the trapdoor. "Probably not."

Lazarus does not point out the obvious. If he had just kept his anger in check, the Singer would not have seen his black teeth or forked tongue.

It's just so difficult to hide the devil's beauty. It's meant to be seen—even by angels.

Tessa

The two men move away from the hall, and Tessa sinks more deeply into the shadows of the room where she's hiding.

Who are those two? And why in the hell would Singers hurt another Singer?

She's confused, but in her twenty years of running, Tessa has learned to stay out of business that's not her own.

She bites her lip. Tessa doesn't like repaying hospitality with silence. There's got to be someone in charge who should know what she saw. Tessa paces out of the shadows.

She's thinking of staying for a couple of days and making sure Tahlia gets picked up by the Lanarre. Then after she's foraged for whatever supplies they'll allow her to take, she'll mention the guy the newest Singers chucked down the chute.

What if the Singer is hurt? Fatally wounded? It feels wrong not to divulge this bit.

Shut up, Tessa. Not your gig, you're a Were for moon's sake.

"Hey," Tahlia says from behind her, and Tessa jumps, hand to her chest.

"Moon! You scared the shit out of me!"

Tahlia grins. "I do adore your expressions. There's no poo anywhere. Yet, you say there is."

"Cut the crap," Tessa grumps.

Tahlia shakes her head, her smile widening. "No, I think you have a fixation with excrement."

Maybe. Tessa scowls, crossing her arms. "What are you doing lurking around here?"

The girl's eyes are round and innocent. Tessa gets a sudden image of her talons ripping out the Were's eyeballs.

Not so innocent.

Tessa might bust if she doesn't tell someone.

Tahlia smells the story before Tessa speaks. "Tell me, Tessa."

Tessa does, and Tahlia's expression mirrors Tessa's thoughts.

She doesn't reply right away. Instead, she jerks her head to the side, and Tessa follows her into a long, narrow room small enough to be a closet. Adjacent to the kitchen, it's lined with cabinets with glass fronts. Fine dishes are stacked inside.

Tahlia shuts the door behind Tessa, then palms behind her butt, she leans against the solid wood.

"Promise me you will say nothing until we depart this place." Her large dark bluish-violet eyes don't look away, compelling Tessa to say yes.

She frowns. "I don't know," she answers slowly. "They've taken us in."

Tahlia gives a small shrug. "I am grateful. But this thing you witnessed? It is a Singer matter. They are not even Were."

She's right, of course.

Still, it feels wrong. Tessa worries at her bottom lip. "Some share our blood."

Tahlia folds her arms, lifting a shoulder. "Not Were enough to change, not Lycan enough to count."

Tessa's gaze narrows on the younger girl.

"That's cold."

Tahlia's chin lifts. "It's the truth, and you know it."

Tessa nods. She does know it but can't shake the feeling of wrongness. "I can tell the Rare One."

Tahlia grabs her arms as Tessa turns to leave. "When we leave this place. No sooner."

"What about the guys? The new Singers." *Especially the blond one.* He was kind of cute before he put the drop on the Singer.

What is wrong with me?

Tahlia's hand falls. "It shows they're capable of violence for its own sake."

Tessa nods. "Yes, it does."

"Simple. We avoid them."

Thalia gives her a sharp look. "You haven't told everyone about me, have you?"

"Enough," Tessa admits. It's sort of important everyone knows she's Lycan royalty. It's not something to screw with.

Tahlia rolls her eyes.

"Well forgive me, your highness, but it was top on the list to find some sanctuary."

Tahlia strips a hairband from her wrist and twists her curly hair into a topknot at the crown of her head. Her eyes find Tessa again. "Not much of a sanctuary if Singers are willing to beat and hide their host in a hole."

That was Tessa's thought, but she won't say it aloud. Instead, she says, "It's a helluva sight better than Tramack getting his paws on me." The reconciliation feels weak.

"Why is he so bad?" Tahlia cocks her head. "Why not mate with him and avoid all this chasing?"

Tessa's abrupt laugh echoes in the small butler's pantry.

"I am *not* Lanarre." Tessa stabs a thumb into her chest. "I wasn't groomed to be mated with some unseen male."

Tahlia's expression moves to hurt, but Tessa doesn't pause. "I want to choose a male who complements me. Who I actually *want*."

A tear struggles out of her burning duct, then another follows.

"Don't you see? I am a prisoner if I stay with the Western pack."

"And now we're just murderers," Tahlia says, her hands slapping her jean-clad thighs.

Shame burns through Tessa. "Yes," she hisses defiantly. "I am guilty of murder. Many times over. And they are guilty of robbing me of my freedom."

"I am guilty of it, as well."

Tessa steps into Tahlia's space. "Then why did you help me? If you are so dead-set on being 'owned,' why would you help me?"

Tessa searches her midnight blue eyes.

"Maybe I want you to be free because I never will be."

Tessa jerks back as though she's been slapped.

"What?" she whispers.

Tahlia wrinkles her nose, and Tessa realizes she's in quarter-change form, subtly breathing in available scents.

"You heard me," Tahlia whispers, ending the conversation as she turns and jerks open the door.

She'd heard her all right. And there was no way to un-hear her.

Tahlia felt as trapped by convention as Tessa did. But unlike Tessa, Tahlia gave up hope.

Tahlia doesn't fight for herself.

But she'd fought for Tessa. It's what she *could* do.

Loyalty doesn't go unnoticed by Tessa. It's such a rare commodity. Servitude won't be over just because the Lanarre come to collect Tahlia.

It'll be over when Tessa thinks it is—and not a minute sooner.

Julia

"*W*hat the hell was *that*?"

Julia backs up and bumps into Scott. His hands grip her shoulders to steady her.

Tharell rises, unbound, with Delilah in his arms. Scott moves protectively in front of Julia.

Tharell takes in Scott's stance. "I do not plan to injure the Blooded Queen."

"Uh-huh," Scott says, disbelief thick in his voice.

Delilah stirs, and Tharell caresses her face.

"What did you do to her?" Julia asks, her eyes bouncing from the wounds at Delilah's throat to the incisors that have sprouted inside Tharell's mouth.

"It is she that did 'something.'"

"Well, shit," Scott says.

"Yup," Julia agrees. She looks around. *First things first.* "Who attacked you?"

Tharell shrugs. "It is someone who is invisible to me."

"Illusionist?" Scott asks.

Julia paces away, casting a glance at Delilah. "So someone comes in here, cuts away your bindings…"

"I did that."

Julia whirls around to face him. "What?"

Tharell smiles, and Julia shivers at the sight of the perfect bead of blood seated on top of his cupid's bow.

Tharell rolls his shoulders in dismissal. They move awkwardly as he holds Delilah. "I could escape at any time. Only iron bonds could hold me. And even you are not as cruel as that."

Julia frowns at his choice of words, ignoring the implication. "I heard it acts like an acid."

Tharell nods.

"Why is Delilah so out of it?" Scott asks, stroking Julia's shoulder. It's so natural to have him touching her, but not without a price. Julia tries to wipe thoughts of Jason from her mind, but she can't quite do it. Scott gives her a sidelong glance. She's not entirely sure how the meld works, only that he's getting leakage.

"Blood exchange." Tharell's lips quirk, his answer breaking though her morose contemplations. "That is my supposition. To be honest"—he smirks—"I did not know that any part of me was vampire. I should, in theory, have been 'found out' during my one thousand years in the sithen—in faerie." Tharell widens his stance, shifting Delilah's slight weight. He lifts his chin.

"Vampires are the fey's mortal enemies. As I have mentioned previously, they bring true death."

Julia stands slightly behind Scott's broad back as he folds his arms. "So how did you manage, having vampire blood when they're the only supes who can do you guys in?"

"I do not know."

"You're not knowing a helluva a lot," Scott says.

Blue eyes unflinchingly regard brown. "True."

"How come *you're* not all noodling out right now?" Julia asks.

Tharell smiles. "I assume you mean why have I not lost control over my senses?"

Delilah's arm takes that opportunity to dangle. Tharell absently tucks it back inside his tight embrace.

Ahh. "Yeah," Julia says, her eyes pegged on the gesture.

"Unlike the other supernatural groups, the fey know the history of all. We make a point of learning."

Scott grunts.

"You have a vampire here. You might ask Brynn if there is validity to my suppositions. My understanding is when a female and male vampire come together in blood exchange, it leaves the female vulnerable. The male remains alert to defend her against all comers. In this way, he fulfills his duty as the stronger of the two, protecting the weaker."

"Makes sense," Scott says.

Julia's brow cinches and she gives him a sharp look, pinching the bridge of her nose. Her brain hurts. "Okay. Say that's true. How was Delilah to know that you wouldn't hurt her?"

"She did not. Delilah only knew that she would heal my injuries with her blood. I have so little vampire genetics that she must have been unaware. As I was."

Scott palms his chin. "Maybe she *was* aware. I thought she agreed to take your ass back to faerie awfully quick."

Tharell moves forward, and Scott tucks Julia behind him tighter. "It's okay, Scott. He wants to go back, not hurt us. If he released his bonds, he could have done whatever."

"Your magick will not contain me this close to faerie. Your lock manipulator cannot change the magick of faerie, not when the music of the sithen plays. However distant its melody, it is just for me."

"And me," Domiatri says in a droll voice from the door.

Tharell's head whips to the warrior he fought beside for centuries, whom he decapitated while under the pull of the demonic.

The air grows heavy—full.

"It's a symphony for me."

Tharell's brows jump above his icy-blue gaze. "Well, wonderful for you, Domiatri."

A staring match ensues, and Julia speaks in the middle of it. "Listen, Domi, I didn't want you to find out like this, but someone…"

She gives Domi an inquisitive look.

"It was not he who put the hole inside my body," Tharell says.

Julia's shoulders slump in relief. She would have to act if Domi had defied their joint decision to hold Tharell.

"How do you know—brother." Domi says *brother* like *fucker*. Julia hears it plain as day.

So does Tharell.

"Because I know that however much you hate me for my actions, to come to me in stealth rather than in plain sight would go against everything you are."

"It would," Domi states. His jaw clenches defiantly.

Julia's brows come together. "Then who hurt you?"

"Who cares?" Domi says.

"Who, indeed?" Tharell agrees severely.

"I do," Delilah says from his arms.

Tharell's face slips into a tender expression before he checks it.

"Can you stand?" Tharell asks gently.

"I think so," Delilah replies.

He sets her carefully on her feet. The brutal splash of blood over her skirt has mucked the area where her knees are underneath the layers of fabric.

Julia's throat convulses. *Gross.*

"Okay—" Julia begins.

Domi interrupts harshly, "What have you done?"

Domi looks from Delilah's healing throat to the new fangs Tharell seems to have suddenly have trouble hiding. "What came naturally?"

Jacqueline rushes in behind Domi, and he stays her with a hand.

Julia gasps at the size of her belly. "What on earth is going on?" she asks Jacqueline.

Jacqueline ignores her. "What is—oh my."

That's so it.

Jacqueline's eyes take in a pale Delilah leaning against the much taller Tharell. Her fingers loosely wrap his forearm as it crosses her chest and he pins her against his body.

The scar at his throat is gone.

Julia glances at Domi. His scar is no longer there, either. *Amazing.*

"It appears as though Tharell is more mongrel than even I knew. He has taken blood from your vampire daughter." Silently, he meets Tharell's gaze.

"Blood exchange?"

Tharell nods.

"Really," Jacqueline breathes out, her hand absently going to stroke the swell of her body.

"What now?" Scott asks.

"It doesn't really change things," Julia says, "except that—*God*, Tharell's a vampire. I want Brynn here. He can tell us more."

"Tharell cannot go back to faerie. He must atone—"

"There is *no* atonement, Domiatri. I will be put to true death once I arrive. But to stay outside"—Tharell grips Delilah more tightly—"is insanity."

Domi scowls. "*This* is insanity." His hand gestures to Delilah.

"I thought, since the fey and vampires are natural enemies, that Delilah would be the best choice to get Tharell back to faerie," Julia explains.

Domi turns the silver of his laser stare at Julia. She swears it burns.

"Why?" he barks at her.

Scott steps between them. "Watch it green man, or I'll see if your guts match your skin."

"Scott," Julia begins.

"Nope. He doesn't get to talk to you like that."

Domi and Scott stare each other down, then Jacqueline rests her hand on Domi's arm. He flicks his eyes at her touch, and Julia watches him build himself anew, into something more reasonable.

"You are right," Domi concedes. "I am—this entire *murder* situation has been distressing."

Distressing? Uh, yeah.

Julia nods. I guess when you've lived a thousand years, an attempt on your life just isn't that important.

"Wow," Delilah says.

Julia ignores Domi and walks to her. They're about the same height, so she meets eyes that are so like Scott's she has to remind herself they just found each other. Technically, they're *half* siblings.

"Wow—what?"

"She has never exchanged blood," Tharell appears to guess.

Delilah pushes away and staggers forward. Tharell catches her with a blinding swipe of speed.

Julia gasps, jumping backward. "Holy crap! I didn't see your arm move!"

"Yes. An advantage of the vampiric, apparently."

Delilah rolls her eyes but doesn't make a second move to get away. "Of *course* I've taken blood from a male before."

Tharell's brows come together.

Delilah folds her arms. "I suppose you think you're so vital that I'm just blown away. You don't suppose it has anything to do with the Heinz 57 that I am? If I've taken from a pure vamp, it just—well it didn't feel the same."

Tharell's expression turns smug.

Delilah huffs, crossing her arms. The blood moving up the sleeves is distracting. "Your penis—did it just grow or something?"

Tharell blanches and Scott snorts.

They glare at each other. "Because unless *that* happened," Delilah continues with slow deliberation, "you shouldn't be behaving as though you are the second coming of Christ."

Tharell flinches at the name of God. Demonic blood is more than blue liquid that runs inside black veins.

There are qualities to it, like there are distinctive elements inherent to her own blood.

Domi dismisses the sparring with an easy hand whip in the air. "Tharell will be executed in faerie."

Julia turns to him, and Jacqueline is unusually quiet.

Julia says, "I can't have him here. Most of my people didn't want him alive. And obviously, someone tried to kill him in secret, against my express order—which we all agreed on. Tharell fought in a battle that killed many of the Region Two Singers. He wasn't here when Tony—when Tony did what he did."

Jacqueline moves deeper into Domi's tall body. He wraps an arm around her shoulder.

The mention of Tony's name was enough to make her shy from it.

Julia understands—too well. "Then there's Tharell making a deal with Gabriel."

Julia shifts her accusing gaze away from Tharell and looks at the others. "We need him to go. And if Delilah could get Tharell to faerie unharmed herself, he would be the fey's problem. Not mine."

Tharell claps. "Well done, Julia."

Julia lets go of a hard sigh. "Listen. I don't have great choices here. My soul-meld with Scott is back. My people are dead. Jason is pissed at me. And you're some kind of new vamp."

"And that's a new item on the agenda. Soul-whatever?" Delilah asks, glancing at Scott.

Julia ignores her. "If Tharell can return to faerie, along with you and Jacqueline, all the fey people will be back where they belong and I can begin to rebuild Region One with who's left."

"And if I refuse?" Delilah asks and Scott's eyes narrow, but he makes no move to leave Julia's side.

Tharell turns Delilah's face to his with a soft touch to her chin. "Would you deny what is between us."

Delilah jerks her chin out of his grasp. "Yes," she hisses. "A little blood bind doesn't mean we're getting married, Sidhe. I never forget that you are fey."

Tharell's hand slowly drops and Julia can't read his expression.

Bad.

"But I concede I'm the logical choice to get your criminal rear end back to the mound. I can do it—Brynn could as well."

"Brynn is pure vampire, the sithen will not allow him inside."

Delilah's face thins to feral sharp, a slight tremor can be seen in a shaky hand as she swipes a stray hair away. "*I* can. I did kill Queen Darcel, if you remember."

"Unforgettable," Domi says in quiet consideration.

"Thank you, Delilah," Tharell says, changing tactics.

Her eyes narrow to slits. "You're welcome, Tharell of the Unseelie."

He gives a little bow then uses his newly acquired vampire speed to jerk her to him.

Delilah yelps in surprise and Tharell gasps as her talons plug him, the tips exiting out of the wound she just healed.

"That is not the way to thank a woman."

Tharell's pain-filled gaze moves to hers. "Then enlighten me."

Delilah jerks the talons out of his body and Tharell slumps forward. "Next time you bite me—you ask."

Tharell's breaths come fast and hard, his body using what energy he gained from the first blood-letting to assist with the new wound.

But Tharell does not heal himself. Instead, his fingers trail a pathway of chemistry so obvious its flame to flesh. The delicate touch runs from Delilah's cheekbone to jaw and her breath catches.

Delilah's vein at her throat rises to the surface under his fingertips like a succulent rope and her heartbeat pushes the lush pulse like a magnet to his touch.

Tharell's gaze latches onto the precious blood source where his fingers rest.

Scott moves Julia behind him again.

A pin could be heard if one were to drop.

"May I?" Tharell asks, but his lips already hover above her throat, his strong hand craning her jaw so the long line of her neck is exposed, his prior wounds stand as twin stark holes against snowy flesh.

Julia can see the immense strength in that grip. Tharell could snap her neck. Instead, he cradles her head as if it were a revered and fragile egg. Five spots of scarlet spread in a red pool at his back where her talons speared him

"You may, you insufferable hybrid."

Tharell's lips twitch as he strikes before any of them can take their next breath.

Delilah doesn't flinch. Instead, she relaxes into his embrace.

When Brynn enters the barn no one hears him.

He attacks Tharell in a smear of rolling bodies. The movement also tears out half of Delilah's throat.

Jacqueline screams and moves to go to her daughter.

Domi seizes her, swinging the mother of his child away from the fray.

Scott likewise holds Julia.

I can't breathe.

Brynn knocks his fist into Tharell, and the Sidhe vampire catches the strike. Tharell's wounds close as Julia watches their movements, their clothing like spinning streamers.

Tharell leverages the fist meant for him and tosses Brynn into the concrete wall behind him. The building shakes from the impact.

"Brynn!" Julia screams.

"No," Scott says, "Yo—you're *so* not going near them."

Brynn rolls away from the concrete wall gracefully, and Julia gasps when she sees the indent of where his body struck the cement.

Julia points to Delilah, but Scott is unyielding armor around her.

Delilah grabs at her throat, eyes wide, gurgling.

Brynn leaps beside her, scooping her off the cold floor. His eyes move to Tharell. "Stay back, newling. You've done enough damage."

Tharell surges forward.

"Tharell! No, wait," Julia cries.

Brynn ignores everyone. His attention is only for Delilah as she drowns in her own blood.

"Shh, you will live, young female." Her flailing arms find his shoulders and latch on.

Brynn grits his teeth against the strength of her hold and folds the mutilated flap of flesh back against her throat.

Delilah bucks, starved for air.

Brynn tears at his wrist. Then balancing her head on his knees, he squeezes the blood out drop by drop.

Her mouth opens, and his dark lifeblood drips inside. Delilah's eyes close. She begins to make mewling sounds like a kitten with its first saucer of cream.

Delilah grabs the wrist above her and latches on with a contented sigh.

Brynn gives Tharell a look of unadulterated disdain. "That is *how* it's done, infant."

Tharell squats beside them. "I am not an infant, and if you do not disengage yourself from her mouth, I will put my fist through your head."

Brynn smirks. "You will try."

Unreal.

"We don't have time for this," Julia says.

"Nope, let them figure this out, Julia. Sometimes men just have to beat the shit out of each other to make sense of it all," Scott says.

That's so illogical.

Neither of them acknowledges Julia or Scott. They're too busy with their testosterone-laden stare fest.

"It is I who saved her. You're too much of a novice to release her from the feed when another vampire attacks. You almost killed a helpless female as she entrusted you to feed from her vein. You. Are. An. Infant."

Tharell's eyes are like dead marbles in his face. "And you shall die if you don't take your wrist from her mouth."

Delilah ends the argument when she releases Brynn, wiping her mouth with the back of her hand.

There aren't many blood-free spots on Delilah anymore. Brynn and Tharell look down at her at the same moment.

She glares at them both. "That hurt like hell."

Looks like they've bitten off more than they can chew.

Literally.

19

Drek- Lanarre prince

"This is absurd."

"They're dead, Drek."

"I can see that." Drek holds out his palm, where congealed blood collects.

"The human law enforcement has already combed the establishment."

Drek's eyebrows lift. "And?"

"They have found nothing we didn't want them to. The human guardians were in bad shape."

"Eviscerated."

"Yes," Bowen answers tersely.

Drek shoots out an exhale like a bullet. "And Tahlia is out there somewhere—a Lanarre princess, unguarded."

"She is skilled, Drek."

He whirls on his trusted guard. "I'm aware she is skilled. However, she will be my queen, Bowen."

"I understand."

Drek kicks the cheap bamboo couch in the hotel room. It flips then hits the wall so hard that the peg legs embed into the drywall.

The room still bears her scent, which is strongest in the bathroom. Drek walks the length of the room and passes through the narrow bathroom threshold.

A faucet drips loudly. Drek has never wished more to change to wolfen than he does in this moment.

He could be so much more aware.

But a seven-foot-tall wolfen will attract too much attention. As it is, it's taken all they could manage to get inside the room without alerting the authorities of their presence.

What I wouldn't give for my wolfen snout—or animal's eyes. Without them he has only his slightly heightened human senses.

Then his eyes catch something that's fallen behind the dingy commode.

It looks like snow.

No—it's a feather. A pure white feather. And balanced on top, is a drop of blood.

Drek stands so quickly his head spins.

"Bowen!" he yells.

Bowen rushes inside, hands gripping the doorjamb. "What is it?"

"She changed into bird form."

They come to the same realization simultaneously.

"She lives."

His gaze moves to the small bathroom window above the shower stall. The window stands open. The opening is just large enough for a bird to move through.

"Yes," Drek answers, clutching the feather.

It breaks under his grip.

Slash

"Hey," Adrianna calls out softly.

Slash jerks up from the ground in a semi-pushup leap. His black nylon athletic pants leave little to the imagination, and he watches Adrianna take that in: his lack of shirt—and underwear.

It's simply not practical for him to be wolfen and not have pants that accommodate his increased girth. Underwear would literally strangle his nuts. The athletic pants are the best he can do, and they're more modest than anything most would partake in.

"What are you doing?" she asks.

Slash can't resist a small chuff to scent her.

Adrianna is nervous. Her emotions fuel a quick scan of the environment.

"Nothing's wrong Slash. I'm just—I'm seeing how you're doing. You've been gone all day."

He moves toward her.

Fear washes over her features.

Slash stops, stunned. "Are you afraid of me?"

Adrianna quickly shakes her head. "No. But, you're big in wolfen form."

He grins. He forgot what he looks like. For a full second, he forgot about his scar.

His smile disappears at the thought but Adrianna is already slipping her arms around his waist, nuzzling against the downy hair that covers his body in this form.

His hand awkwardly cups her small skull, and he thinks of all of what he loves contained in the fragile container of her head. He swallows painfully.

She is so vulnerable. And he can think of nothing else but her protection.

He voices different thoughts, though. "Julia tasked me with scenting the dead."

Adrianna tips her head back. "Kind of shitty."

Slash shakes his head as his mouth pulls into a thin smile and flattens his scar. "No. It must be done. I'm a pureblood Red. Truman, Zeke, and I are making short work of it."

Adrianna looks out over the small lake then glances at her feet.

Slash nods. "The fey were able to get all the…pieces."

Adrianna nods at the word for the torn bodies of the dead.

"They put them in a mass grave. It's up to us to exhaust the tally of fallen Were."

Understanding lights her expression. "Lawrence."

Slash nods, unable to tell her just how selfish his motivation is. The packmaster is the one true obstacle standing between Slash's union with Adrianna.

"If he's gone, then we can be together."

Emotion overcomes him and Slash can't keep form and bleeds to human.

The short coat of red hair that covers his body disappears and only the barest grunt whistles out of him as he shrinks to the shorter stature of six foot four.

Adrianna is still her fierce tiny package of female.

Slash moves his fingers beneath her jaw and tilts it up, looking deeply into her eyes.

"Adrianna."

Her lips twist. "Just kiss me. I'm dying here."

A hint of a smile pulls his mouth, and then it's on hers. Slash has been with many females.

They never saw his face; he made sure of it.

He never loved them, but a male has needs.

But everything he needs is now here inside his arms.

The sunlight warms his face and sparkles off the water.

It showcases his scar.

Yet, he allows Adrianna to pull him down to meet her soft lips.

Slash is not starved for sex, but love is a different matter. And Slash knows that sex will be consuming when love is a part of it.

And he loves Adrianna so much, it's a type of sweet agony.

It hurts him deeply because he gave up some of his self-preservation to feel it.

Then her small hands slide just underneath the waistband of his pants and Slash is lost to her touch.

Just lost.

———

Slash leads Adrianna by the hand. The woods deepen around them. The trees grow thicker and broader.

"I'll be cold, Slash," Adrianna says with just a touch of coyness to her voice.

But she does not say no.

"Let my body warm you," he says.

She lifts his hand and kisses each knuckle, never looking away.

Slash sucks in a breath. "Lawrence is dead," he confesses.

"I thought he might be," she says, giving a significant look around the woods. "You wouldn't take me as mate unless he was out of the picture."

Slash smiles, and Adrianna grins back.

"How do you know I am taking you as mate?" he teases.

Adrianna's hand is suddenly cupping his balls, and he gasps. "You better be, buster. I'm not doing the nasty with just anyone."

Slash seizes her wrist. "You are mine. There will be no other who knows your body, Adrianna."

A slow smile spreads across her full lips, and her hazel eyes sparkle. "Just the way I want it, stud. Now let me do something more fun with these."

Slash isn't shy, but when the one woman he loves has him by the balls, it's a strange position to be in.

"Adrianna," he calls softly as her fingers cup him intimately.

"Yeah," she replies. Her half-hooded eyes widen slightly. "I know what you're going to ask."

"Then you know it will be better in quarter-change."

She nods. "I'm young, not dumb."

Slash wants her. Badly.

He doesn't want to hurt her, but he will. There is no reversing it. Virginity is the one thing that unifies all the species. Females who are pure will experience pain at the loss of it.

Slash takes her in his arms. "I would do anything to spare you."

"Slash, stop. I've always wanted you. I couldn't *do this* with anyone else."

Slash growls.

Adrianna's eyebrows pop. "Don't go all Alpha on me."

Slash doesn't answer. He bends over, taking her earlobe deeply inside his mouth and nips it, drawing blood.

Adrianna whimpers.

Slash hardens against her. "You can't go back, Adriana. Once we are mated, whatever I have is yours. Whatever I lack, will remain."

Her hand moves to him again, gently squeezing and he groans.

"You lack nothing," she whispers.

Adrianna kisses what she can reach, moving her lips across his unscarred chest. His nipples harden inside the cool interior of the woods.

"Where are the guys?" she asks against his hot skin.

"They won't disturb us."

"Better not," she says, giving his nipple a hard nip.

Slash pulls a sharp inhale that's a half-moan.

"Don't, Adrianna."

"Were like teeth," she says as though reading from a textbook.

"Perhaps too much," Slash says, knowing where that can lead.

Adrianna takes his pants down to his ankles.

Slash stands before her, unashamed by his nudity, hoping she forgives his face for what his body offers.

Adrianna stares at him silently for so long he can't fight the heat that spreads from his neck to settle at his face. He physically restrains himself from jerking the pants back on and walking off.

Adrianna finally looks at his face, which only makes his shame burn brighter.

"You are the most beautiful man I've ever seen." Her lips part, a flush rivaling his own spreads across her cheekbones and Slash's nostrils flare at her arousal.

Slash grins so he won't cry and grabs her in a hug so fierce she taps out on his shoulder.

He pulls away, and her face is purple.

"Maybe a little too tight," she squeezes out, her fingers barely apart.

Slash can't stop smiling. Adrianna called him beautiful.

Then she takes off her clothes, and Slash knows his beauty is merely a shadow of hers.

20

Julia

"No, absolutely not." Julia looks from Brynn to Tharell, then her gaze goes to Delilah. "I asked you to go with Tharell. Back when he was a fey-slash-demonic. Now he's a vamp?" Julia throws up her hands, and they slap down on her thighs.

"And can I mention, for the record, that you guys shouldn't even be standing with all the blood that's lying around?" Julia crosses her arms, fuming.

"Julia."

She turns reluctantly to Scott.

His eyes beseech her to listen.

"Brynn was William's second, right?"

She throws a look at Brynn. "Yes," she answers slowly, "after he was tortured at Merlin's orders, Brynn and the handful of other vamps are all who survived." It's important to clarify everything.

Scott nods. "Okay, so he's the only vamp around that you trust."

Julia supposes that's accurate. "Yeah."

"Delilah's already decided to go. Brynn can supervise. Two vamps against the big bad fey."

Scott winks at her and Julia steps into his arms and hugs him around the waist. "You're *so* funny."

He strokes her back. "I know."

"Hmm," she says against him, but she's smiling.

"Tharell can do nothing to us. Two against one. Plus," Brynn says, "it's against vampire nature to kill or harm a female. And it's not about gallantry, Julia."

"What is it then?" she asks, frowning as she tosses Tharell a surreptitious glance. Disgruntled doesn't cover it.

"It's about self-preservation. If the males are chasing around and killing all the females, where do the new vampires come from. Offspring."

Jason strolls into the open barn door, hands stuffed inside his pockets, his gaze moving to where Julia stands beside Scott. "Don't you just latch onto someone new and change them, blood sucker?"

He smirks.

Great, Jason's going to be himself, when we really need this. Tharell needs to get gone so tempers can cool.

Scott takes her hand, and Julia tries to pull away, though she wants nothing more than to collapse against him in relief.

Jason notices the subtle tug-of-war and his smug expression turns to the hard edges of rage.

Julia is intimately familiar with that expression. Julia stops struggling. She is the rope between two men, and she's fraying quickly.

Brynn glances between all of them. "Yes, we *can* change some humans into vampires, but they must already be vampiric. They must have the blood of a vampire to change." He glances at Tharell. "As the Sidhe warrior did."

Jason's eyebrows hike. "Really? So Tharell's gone all vampy. Well, isn't this just fucked."

Jason's got it right. It's a mess.

"So"—Jason taps his chin—"let me get this straight, as I've just been invited to this little party." When his eyes find Julia's, she doesn't look away. "You three vamps are going to the fey mound, and you'll take your chances there." His eyes move to Delilah's still-healing neck, and he checks a snort. "And Tharell is going to hope the fey just welcome him back with open arms? Not fucking likely."

Jason walks slowly over to Julia and Scott. His eyes rake down her body then move back to her face.

"And Julia's all entangled with Singer royalty again, while battling a demonic spore."

Jacqueline glances at Julia and she casts her eyes to the floor.

"Is this true, Julia?"

"Yes." She gives a sharp exhale. "The saber—the demonic blood can't kill me, but I'll just get sicker."

"Until a high demon comes along and finds Jules. Then he can do her in." Jason looks at her coldly, but Julia knows it's his anger talking. He's angry she'll grow sick, and the situation with Scott has only renewed that rage.

Jason licks his lips. "All Jules has to do is hook up with Scott here, and the high demon can pack sand, right, guys?"

Julia's miserable. A few short years ago, she couldn't envision a life without Jason.

Now she knows that'll never happen.

Brynn fills the awkward silence. "Then it would make sense for Tharell to be gone from here, so if the demonic return, he can't be commanded to act on any direction given by them."

"Won't he be too vampire to be driven by demonic directives?" Jacqueline asks.

"I think demonic trumps vamp," Julia guesses.

"I know it does," Domi says.

Jason turns to Brynn, Delilah, and Tharell. "Then you better go. Because even though I'd love to kick some ass, I don't want one chance for some devil guys showing up and hurting Jules."

"But *you* are allowed to hurt her by staying?" Tharell asks, getting to the heart of it.

Jason smiles and it's more a baring of teeth. "Yeah. I've earned the right, purple dick."

Tharell moves in a streak of lavender. He slams Jason against the wall, holding his hand at Jason's throat. "Courtesy, Were."

"Fuck you, grape."

Julia runs to them. Scott reaches to grab her.

No, please, Scott.

He stills at her telepathic missive.

Be careful.

She turns and puts her hand on Tharell. "Please, just go. Don't harm Delilah."

Tharell looks down at her, his fingers like steel at Jason's throat. "I will die inside faerie."

Julia squeezes her eyes shut. "You will die here."

"I know."

Julia opens her eyes and watches as Tharell drops Jason. He massages his throat then looks at Julia.

She lowers her eyes before what she sees in his, feeling sick.

"I'll get my shit. It seems to me you have plenty of protectors here, Jules. I'm just in the way."

Julia grabs him, latching onto his arms. He flings his arms wide and her hands fly backward. "Don't," he snarls.

Scott is suddenly in front of her. "It's all about you, Caldwell."

Jason's eyes are all for Julia.

"Not always."

Jason stalks off, not giving anyone anything but his back and the dust off his feet.

⟋⟍⟍

Thankfully, Delilah has time to put on fresh clothes for the journey to the mound. They didn't announce her departure.

Brynn and Tharell wait at the stand of trees that bisect the lake from Highway 101. The mound is beyond even that, west toward the Olympic Mountains at the edges of the Hoh Rain Forest.

"I feel bad," Julia says, reaching for Delilah's hand. "I know we're not close, that we don't even really know each other."

"It's fine." Delilah gingerly lays a hand on her throat, where the faint scarring is nearly healed.

Julia breathes a sigh of relief.

I think we'll have to do a hazmat clean of the barn floor. She shudders at the recent memory.

"It changes things," Julia says.

Delilah nods. "It does. I know he could kill me if the right devil shows up." The corner of Delilah's mouth lifts.

"Not. Funny," Julia says but she laughs.

"Nothing is certain, Julia—that's why Brynn is going."

"Another complication—"

"A contingency," she interrupts.

Neither one of them mention Brynn's actions in saving Delilah in what looked like an attack by Tharell. *Protective vampire instinct or something else?*

Julia shoves her hair behind her ears. Her head hurts with all the thoughts piling up inside it.

Delilah shrugs. "I'll be fine."

"You're still a girl—like me."

"A woman who killed the Queen of the Unseelie."

A shaky laugh escapes Julia. "Right. I know."

"*You* requested I take him."

Julia stares into Delilah's black gaze. "*Before* Tharell vamped out."

Delilah crosses her arms. "Brynn and I will return. Once Tharell enters the sithen, he is a problem for the fey. Not us."

"It's like a death sentence."

"It's as you said. He waits, demons will come, and then he is an addition to the army."

"A possible addition."

Neither of them enumerates the possibilities of how that particular event could spin out.

"True. However, this gets him away from whoever usurped your authority."

Dissent in the ranks.

Julia throws up her hands. "Okay, you win."

"Of course." Delilah grins, and the dimple she shares with Scott winks in and out of existence.

"What about Jacqueline?"

Delilah sighs. "I'm not sure which I like better," she admits quietly. "This soft, pregnant Jacqueline or the tough monarch."

Julia jerks back. "What? Jacqueline without the moderation of faerie tried to murder me. She was a bitch on wheels."

Delilah nods. "Yes, but a little bit of that is needed now. And she's just too broken to give that side of herself. What if something horrible happens? And you need what Jacqueline can bring?"

"I think she'll rise to the occasion."

Delilah gives a quick nod, looking over Julia's shoulder. "She's here to see me off."

Julia's mouth makes an *O*, and she turns in the direction Delilah is staring.

Jacqueline moves out of the shadows. Neither Scott nor Domi is in sight.

Julia knows it's an illusion. Domi is protective over Jacqueline.

Scott would never let anything happen to Julia. However, she appreciates the impression of privacy.

"I wished to tell you goodbye."

Delilah lifts a shoulder. "It doesn't matter."

"It does. I have something to tell you. It might make a difference—it might not."

Julia begins to back away, thinking she doesn't need to intrude on their private moment.

"No—stay," Jacqueline says.

Julia stills. Jacqueline's face is so grave, Julia's pretty sure she doesn't want to hear the words that Jacqueline will speak.

"I know that I have been an absent and neglectful mother, as I was with Scott."

Delilah says nothing, and Julia's impressed. Most would rub in the obvious.

Julia studies Delilah's face and comes to the conclusion that maybe her vampire nature offers a sort of natural indifference. If so, Jacqueline can't mend that bridge.

"You have asked, and I have refused."

Julia's ears perk as she looks between the two. *What?*

Delilah's skirts swish at her ankles as she moves forward suddenly. She takes Jacqueline's hands in her own.

"My sire?"

Julia holds her breath as the two women face off. Both are dark and severe as well as cunning.

"He does not know of your existence."

"And I do not know his identity," Delilah replies.

Jacqueline takes a deep inhale, letting it out slowly. "It is Gabriel of the Northwestern Kiss."

Delilah backs away, dropping her mother's hands as though she were burnt. "No."

Julia's breath escapes in a rush that makes her dizzy. Her hand hits the side of the barn.

Delilah is the daughter of a Rare One, the very leader who tried to get into bed with Tharell to reacquire her.

Now his own daughter will travel with Tharell.

"He is merciless!" Delilah cries, and Julia watches Brynn and Tharell make haste to their positions.

"It is a trait I desired in the fathers of my children."

Uh-oh.

Delilah's frantic eyes meet her mother's. "Why?" Her voice is as sharp as a blade.

"Survival of the fittest," Jacqueline admits in a vacant tone.

"For whom?"

Jacqueline's eyes shift to the left.

"For me." Her voice has dropped to a thready whisper.

21

Slash

" *I*'m not playing the role of blushing virgin."

Adrianna is suddenly shy, and of course, that makes Slash go from hard to soft in an instant.

Slash is stalled but not done. In two strides, he stands in front of her.

"Adrianna?"

She glances up at him then away.

"I'm going nowhere."

She takes a deep breath, and he scents her anxiety. He also sees the muscle definition in the tenseness along her thighs.

Slash wraps his hands around her upper arms. "I'll be gentle."

"That's not in question."

"What is it then?"

"Tony."

Slash's hands convulse around her arms.

"He didn't—I thought." Slash touches his forehead to hers. "Tell me he did not do what I'm thinking. Because he'd need to die again."

A sad smile touches her lips then disappears. "No, but it was close—so close, Slash."

"I don't want to harm you, but the first time will hurt."

Her breath is warm against his skin. She's frightened.

Slash can't back down, even now, despite knowing her trepidation.

Her small hands float to his hips, and just like that, he's back to unbearably hard. "Adi," he breathes against her, and his lips are at her temple. "I can't not want you, female."

"I want you, too, Slash."

He bends at the knees, and her hands fall away. Slash glories in the sight of her for a full thirty seconds then scoops her into his arms.

Slash didn't plan on this.

But the moss of the forest is dry. He kicks their small pile of scattered clothes with a single swipe, and they fall on top of the dry spongy floor. He arranges Adrianna on top of the bed of moss and clothes.

Adrianna turns her head, and her nostrils flare, her senses heightened in her quarter-change form. "They smell of you."

Slash's eyes run down the length of her body. Her beauty is subtle—perfect.

TAMARA ROSE BLODGETT

Round breasts fall softly to the sides of her chest, and her ribcage narrows to a waist he can span with his hands. Her hips flare just wide enough of a woman just past whelpling age and far enough to be ready for what Slash offers. His eyes move to her perfect toes, and she wiggles them under his scrutiny.

Her face flames when his eye come to her sex.

"Show me, Adrianna."

Her thighs tremble, but she parts them. Slash falls to his knees to lay the side of his face against the inside of her thigh. His nose is inches from the most secret part of her.

"Am I…" Adrianna's voice shakes, and she clears her throat. "Okay?"

"*Okay* is not a word I would ever use to describe you, Adrianna."

He can feel her heartbeat through her femoral artery.

Slash turns his face, laying a heated breath at her core.

She arches her back, "Slash!" she says in a whisper-shout, grasping his hair with her hand.

"Do you like it?"

"Love," she replies breathlessly.

His voice rumbles against her wet heat, "Do you want more?"

"Is there—more?"

"Yes." He places his hands at the apex of where thigh meets her center, and he spreads her like a flower.

Adrianna tenses.

"Trust me, Adrianna."

"You know I do."

"I will prepare you." Slash waits, and when she relaxes, he moves in deeper between her legs. Using his tongue, Slash begins at one side of her and sucks the sensitive flesh deeply into his mouth.

"Ahh," she says, and fingers that had previously bit into his scalp now rub through the stubble of his hair.

"That's it. Open yourself to me."

Adrianna's knees fall apart, and he tucks his hands underneath her hips, cupping the globes of flesh, lifting as he pulls her more deeply into his mouth.

She whimpers, and he licks her from entrance to clit, using the flat of his tongue to rub back and forth on the sensitive nub. Adrianna begins to make little sounds of pleasure, coming undone from the attention.

Slash's erection is a painful, throbbing mass. He denies himself, giving pleasure to the only female he could ever consider mating. She begins to ride his mouth with eager hips, and he matches her rhythm with his own.

When he pierces her entrance with his tongue, she cries out, and Slash does it again and again, holding her bare ass with one hand as the other strokes her slick clit rapidly with his thumb.

Adrianna's body tenses as her head whips violently back and forth. She screams, her body an arc, and Slash slows his tongue penetration then stops it, carefully lowering her to the soft forest floor.

Her eyes are spinning gold, and every feature of her beautiful face glows in stark relief.

"Take me," she says, and Slash is unsurprised by the growling quality to her voice.

Slash lines himself up with her center.

Adrianna gives silent consent with the widening of her legs, letting her arms fall behind her head. Her generous breasts lift, the nipples pointing at his body.

Slash enters her with a single, hard shove. He tears through her barrier and meets the end of her in a quivering thrust of flesh married.

"Oh my—moon!" Adrianna gasps, struggling not to tense against his entry.

Slash feels horrible, but her slick heat and the way her body welcomes his as though he never left, is too much, and he begins to move gently within her.

His head hangs as he lifts his weight from above her, working deeply in and out. "I am sorry—you are—I am lost in you."

She rocks back against him, "Nope, I have you, Slash."

"You do, every part of me," he whispers with clenched eyes.

His eyes snap open as her hands rest on his hips, guiding him—encouraging him. "Do not. I can't hold back, Adrianna."

"I don't want you to."

He freezes above her, his gaze searching hers in the shadows. "Have I hurt you?"

"Not like I'll hurt you if you stop."

Slash smiles, and she grins back, her teeth very sharp. He begins to move with purpose, using long gentle strokes. She fits him like a hot slick glove as he bottoms out to kiss her womb.

"Take me, take me, take me, Slash."

Slash studies her expression, and when he's satisfied it's what she wants, he does what his body has been longing to do since she came of age. He buries himself to the hilt inside her.

They grunt at the deep joining, and her legs fold over his back. He lifts her hips, tilting them forward as he begins to pound inside of her.

"Please," she whispers, and Slash can hold back no more. She is tight and untried by all but him. He plunges in a final time and unloads his seed into her depths, simultaneously scent-marking her.

She milks him, pulsing around him as she makes little grunts of satisfaction. They are music to his ears. That he could possibly satisfy this female who's entrusted him fills Slash with an unaccustomed sensation.

It's beyond the momentary contentment of this act between them.

Beyond that, he has claimed a mate.

More than fleeting happiness, Slash feels true joy—his and hers.

Their own.

Slash scrolls a fingertip down Adrianna's naked side and watches the trail of gooseflesh rise in its wake.

Adrianna giggles. "Stop. You're tickling me, ya butt."

Slash gives a lazy smile. "Butt, eh?"

Adrianna rolls onto her back, and his hand rests on her naked hip.

Her eyes twinkle. "You're so old, Slash."

His eyebrow raises. There *is* a great span between their ages. "Does that bother you?" Slash asks, hoping it does not because there's no rectifying it. He has taken her as mate.

She raises her hand, and he doesn't flinch when she touches the small unsavory mound of flesh that sits in the center of his upper lip. Instead, he catches her hand with his own and kisses her finger.

A long shuddering sigh eases out of her, and his gaze catches on Adrianna's gorgeous breasts.

"You like looking at me."

Slash's eyes move to her face. "Yes," he admits. "Now that I can, I cannot look away."

"You're a romantic, Slash." There's surprise in her voice. He hears pleasure, too.

His brows quirk and the heat of embarrassment rises to his face.

"Don't deny, buddy—I can tell."

Slash mounds her breasts, and her breath catches, her hazel eyes darkening like the threat of a storm.

"What else can you tell, Adrianna?" he asks softly, never looking away while rolling her pebbled nipple between his thumb and finger.

"I can tell that I want to go again."

Slash smiles, cupping her heat with his other hand, and she spreads her legs.

"Are you sore?" he asks, kissing first one thigh then the inside of the other. He rolls his face against her flesh, taking the skin deep between his teeth, smelling her blood and his seed mingled together.

Ambrosia.

"Not enough," she says in a voice gone low with need.

He releases the flesh of her thigh. His teeth leave indentions, but the skin is unbroken. The marks plump and smooth out as Slash watches.

"The quarter-change is helping to heal me," she says, relief in her voice.

"It was smart, Slash." She laughs, and he looks up from where he just pleasured her to her expressive face. "But I think there was an ulterior motive."

"Oh?" he asks, his fingers caressing her entrance.

"Yes," she says, her voice breathy, "I think you just wanted me as much as you could get."

Slash's fingers stop. He glides up her body, caging Adrianna with his arms, placing his hardness against her soft slit. He cradles her face with his hands, elbows planted on either side of her.

He kisses her forehead, each eyelid, then her mouth.

"Yes."

"Ha! I knew it."

He brushes his lips against hers.

"I knew once I started loving you, once would not be enough."

Adrianna wraps her arms around his neck.

"For me, either," she whispers.

22

Drek

"That was a round about," Bowen snorts, twirling his finger in the air.

"We are Lanarre—we can scent the rain on the wind."

Bowen rolls his eyes.

Drek scowls. "What is that look for?"

"We may be Lanarre, but when Tahlia takes flight, there's no scenting her."

Drek hates to admit any failure, but Bowen is right. If the other Alpha female's ground scent hadn't been nearby, they might have missed Tahlia altogether.

"Interesting scent mix at the gasoline station," Bowen remarks.

Drek gives him a sharp look. About half of all supes, even vampires, could have scented the mess Tahlia made. He didn't know why Tahlia was with another female Were, but he suspected the second female was rogue. Drek understood the implications of an Alpha female running solo. None were good, certainly not once Tahlia was added to the equation.

Did the female help Tahlia?

Drek doubted that. Tahlia's scent was mingled with the blood of the males. That could mean only two things.

They had harmed her and Tahlia had defended herself. That option was highly unlikely. No average Were would harm a Lanarre.

The second option: she had attacked them in defense of another, most likely the second female.

From all reports and his abbreviated correspondence with Tahlia, he suspected the latter to be the most probable.

Drek smiles, palming his chin.

"You've thought of something?" Bowen asks. The Were has been Drek's friend and guard since whelphood. Bowen's family has been the guard of the Lanarre royalty for a thousand years, an anomaly, for they are not human.

"Yes."

Bowen's dark eyebrows rise, his light brown eyes steady on Drek.

"I think she defended the Alpha female."

Understanding lights Bowen's expression. "Good call."

"There's a remote possibility that she was defending herself against the two males." He gives Bowen a sharp look.

He immediately shakes his head. "Absolutely not. A Lanarre female just out of whelp? It'd go against every precept in Lycan culture."

"There's precedence."

Neither of them speak of the scent of the Alpha Were who has murdered over nine humans, including Tahlia's guards.

Bowen lifts a shoulder. "Who knows what that Were was made of? If he was being tasked by a packmaster or acting of his own volition?"

"True." But Drek is troubled. A Were who would rampage through a human establishment like that was capable of other deeds.

He and Bowen exchange an uneasy look. "He would not kill her but might do other unsavory things."

A flutter appears in Bowen's jaw, and voices what has occurred to them both. "He would not rape a Lanarre female. She's barely more than a girl."

Drek's stomach does a slow, heated roll. "He is not Lanarre. It would go against *our* instincts to protect females. But as you've said, we can't be absolutely sure."

Bowen throws his hands up in the middle of the parking lot of the decaying gas station. "Let's run with the assumption that he missed her. That she hid herself. That the slaying of her guardians wasn't for nothing."

Drek's eyebrows jerk up to his hairline. "An Alpha male would scent a Lanarre."

"Not if she was in bird form."

Drek puts his hands to hips and walks off. He paces back and forth. Ignoring the coming dawn and the coolness, he scents the ocean in the distance.

His nose is at the scene, and he can't get out of his head. He whirls and looks at Bowen. "Then we make haste. We scent where their car has gone and follow."

Bowen walks to him then grips him by the arms. Though Bowen is only a fraction shorter, Drek is built for war. All Lanarre are. The royal line is the most barbarically fashioned. Both men stand nearly eye-to-eye at six feet five.

"Don't lose faith. This crazed male missed her once. It's clear Tahlia is now with the Alpha female we presume she helped."

Bowen wrinkles his nose. "Those males were from the Western. Easy to scent."

"Possibly drones sent by Tramack?"

Bowen rolls his shoulders into a dismissive shrug. "I don't keep up on common Were politics."

Drek grins suddenly. "And you accuse me of being a snob?"

"Ha!" Bowen replies, dropping his hands from Drek's arms and walking toward the gas pumps. "No accusation necessary. You're an elitist."

Drek can't deny it—the common dens don't adhere to the ways of Lycan tradition enough to earn his respect. A few dens still cleave to the traditions of old, but they are few and far between.

Bowen drops to his hands and knees on the ground, dirtying the knees of his well-worn jeans. He turns his face and hovers above the damp asphalt. He flares his nostrils once then makes several small chuffs.

His head snaps up.

"I have it."

Metal is especially hard to scent, but Bowen has made a little game of it. He can usually get the decade of a vehicle from scent alone. Bowen is good enough at tracking that he can determine what year the car is.

"Older model, 1960s Chevy—heavy."

"They're all heavy from that era," Drek says with a touch of humor. "Really old model."

Bowen rocks back and sits on his heels, nearly yanking his shoulders to his ears. "Perspective. I was a whelp in that day, but you were already thirty-five."

Drek smirks.

"One hundred percent original components," Bowen says triumphantly.

Drek's jaw drops. "Really?"

"Yes, probably an old couple, had it since the day they got married. Grocery-getter for the woman." His eyes glitter. "It happens."

"Rarely."

"Better for us, the signature will be clean to follow."

"What are we waiting for?" Drek says.

Bowen bounds to his feet in a single leap from his toes. "Nothing, let's roll."

Drek gives him a tolerant look. Bowen loves human slang. Drek finds it tiresome, though he's adopted a few key phrases himself.

Drek grits his teeth, angry over the loss of Tahlia's human guardians with an undercurrent of acute anxiety for her. The humans who serve the Lanarre are greatly loyal, with generations upon generations of service.

Drek would dismember the male who slaughtered them if Tahlia hadn't already. Any male who would touch a Lanarre female deserves death. Drek is keenly aware of Tahlia's proficiency in defense. However, she is still female. And judging by the remains of the humans, the male who is responsible for the massacre is strong.

He seems stronger than most Were, but he's not Lanarre-strong. If the male were human, Drek would have assumed he'd been taking some artificial enhancer, like PCP.

Bowen turns, giving Drek a considering look. "Stop thinking. Let's go."

Stop thinking. Easier said than done.

Drek glances over his shoulder, noting the neon sign that reads *gas* switching on.

They'll track during the beginning of day and find Tahlia by nightfall. Drek is optimistic.

Just beyond the tree line, Bowen and Drek morph into quarter-change. The ability that is generally reserved for female Were is available to all Lanarre, male and female. Still, so far from the moon's fullness, the ability comes at a cost to the males.

Bowen and Drek race parallel to the road, following the scent of the car. They slow as the scent stops, then they climb the embankment that leads to the highway. A car passes, and they freeze, waiting for the scent to waft back.

It floats down to rest.

Drek moves to the shoulder, sinking to his haunches. He touches the impression of deep treads biting into the soft dirt and pebbles. He closes his eyes, inhaling deeply.

The car was parked here. Tahlia was inside.

His eyes seek Bowen, but he's already at the edge of the woods.

"I have her."

Drek looks, hoping that Bowen literally has her.

"Her scent, Drek."

Drek's shoulders drop. "I know," he replies and glances behind him.

Two cars were parked at the shoulder. He's scented them both.

Where did the other drivers go? Why were they here, parked behind my chosen? Drek doesn't like it, and he can't dismiss the possibilities of what it represents, especially the scent.

The ones who were here beside the unknown female and his chosen—they are scentless.

Bowen motions impatiently.

"I am a prince, you know," he reminds Bowen.

"Uh-huh, get your princely ass over here so we can find Tahlia."

Drek smirks. "You don't show proper respect, Bowen. And no one cares more about finding Tahlia than I."

Bowen pegs his hands on his hips, one foot in the woods and one on the slope. "And you clearly don't give a shit about anything but finding Tahlia."

Drek grins. "Yes, but we have a problem."

Bowen's brows come together, all humor gone, and his posture tenses. "What?"

"We have scentless followers."

"Vampire?" Bowen asks instantly, his nostrils flaring and a scowl forming on his face. "Can't scent a thing."

"Exactly."

"Doesn't feel right, Drek."

Drek nods. Vamps would avoid daylight for obvious reasons and especially Lycan females. That interaction is a mess waiting to happen. Vampires employ stealth. It is their nature.

No, the followers are not vamps.

Drek studies the impressions at the shoulder again. His eyes move restlessly over every groove or tread. His mind touches on an idea and instantly dismisses it.

There has not been a tangible appearance of cloaked demonic in centuries. There would not be one now.

Still, it strikes a discordant note deep within Drek. He doesn't favor the idea of Tahlia with an unknown female while a deranged Were with a penchant for murdering innocent humans is on the loose. *And now this new potential threat…*

Drek doesn't trust anything he can't scent. No self-respecting Lycan would.

"Drek?" Bowen calls from the bottom of the embankment.

"I don't like it."

Bowen throws his hands up in the air, disbelief saturating his features. "What's to like?"

"These other scentless beings changes nothing," Drek says slowly. Except his chosen is vulnerable and is probably not experienced enough to understand a hidden threat is closing in. She is very young.

Drek jogs down the small hill to the forest's edge to join Bowen, who's already racing ahead of him. They run side by side, shoving aside alder branches like ready whips in front of their faces.

"Wolfen," Bowen gasps.

Their clothes shred. Drek's more prepared than Bowen, who is left in his expandable underwear. Drek specifically chose the plain athletic pants because they would accommodate his change to wolfen form.

The Lanarre all possess coats of silver. A light downy mat of hair like gray smoke covers Bowen as he runs, and Drek knows he looks nearly identical. In wolf form, his coat is tipped in silver but otherwise black. In wolfen form, they both move with power that they could not spare while in quarter-form.

"Wait!" Drek calls, stopping so quickly that he snatches at a trunk to arrest his progress. The tree groans with the impact as his talons punch into the bark. A fine spray of needles falls softly, and the smell of pine is pungent.

Drek flings them out of his hair, but some remain tangled in the fine hairs that cover his body

"What?" Bowen asks, jogging back to Drek's position.

"I scent Blood Singers."

Bowen nods, unsurprised. "This is close to their territory."

Drek inhales deeply, his eyes widening. "Tahlia," he breathes her name reverently.

"How did I miss that?"

"Chasing the ball!" Drek answers with a healthy dose of sarcasm.

Bowen flips him off. "I did *not* ignore scenting to chase the one scent."

Drek snorts, his snout wrinkling. Bowen always has trouble multi-scenting. He gets one scent and gets obsessive.

An irritated exhale rushes out of Bowen. "Okay, maybe a little."

Drek's talons click as is thumb and index come together. "All the way."

"Right—go on," Bowen replies impatiently.

"They're not enemies of the Were," Drek comments significantly. "They would take in two lone Were females."

"Yes," Bowen admits.

"So Tahlia must have found refuge in their territory."

Bowen sighs and shoots a glance Drek's way. "That's a reach."

"I don't believe in coincidence." His eyes lock on the slowly spinning mercury orbs in Bowen's face. "An Alpha female, my chosen, and two Singer males—together?"

"You're right. But this will have to be handled with a degree of diplomacy you lack, Drek."

Drek's face tightens. "I have certain inalienable rights here."

"Of course. But they're a different species, with different rules that govern their kind. We might not be able to just waltz in there with nary a care and grab Tahlia. There might be a protocol in place."

Drek's face whips to Bowen's and he feels his eyes spinning in response to his heightened agitation.

"Fuck protocol."

Bowen's chin dips. "I was afraid you'd say that."

There are no words after that, only speed.

23

Cyn

*C*ynthia folds her arms. "You have *got* to be kidding?"
Jason whirls around, punching the wall. Plaster flakes
float to the floor. "Do I look like I'm fucking kidding?"

Cynthia studies his tense body as if he were a coiled snake.
She sighs. "I'm not gonna lie. This sucks donkey dicks."

Jason snorts. "Yeah."

"What are ya gonna do?"

Cynthia feels for him. He's so raw. The last three years
have been a torture. And in a way, it never stopped. Jason's
been on a perpetual roller-coaster ride like an emotional
junkie with no fix in sight.

"What do you think?" he asks, disdain thick in his
voice.

Cynthia looks down at her feet, momentarily taking
note of her shitty footwear. *Why does that matter?* She

doesn't know, but in this crazy-ass new world of hers, she just wants something cute, goddammit.

Instead, she faces Jason—and reality. "You're going."

He jerks his head in a nod. "Hell, yes. I'm not sticking around to watch Julia do Scott."

"God, that's crude—even for you."

He strides toward her, but Cynthia holds her ground. Jason's volatile, but she doesn't think he'll melt down all over her.

Jason sees something in her and slows, his expression like thunder. "What? You think I'd put my hands on you?"

Cynthia quickly shakes her head. "No, but you're— you're not yourself, Jas—"

"No shit?" He rakes a hand through his sandy hair. "My wife"—he thumbs his chest hard enough to leave a bruise—"is all soul-tied…"

"Meld."

"Whatever-the-fuck!" he roars, and Cynthia's mouth snaps shut.

"With Scott," he spits.

Cynthia's in full-diffusion mode. "Listen, Jason, I know you're freaking out right now…"

His hands clench into fists, his jaw goes hard, and his eyebrows yank in blatant disbelief. "Yeah. Ya think?"

Cynthia blows out a hard breath, crossing her arms. "But you'll never forgive yourself if something happens to Jules."

He meets her eyes, his hazel irises turning green.

"You're not going all wolfy on me, are ya?"

"Maybe."

Cynthia fold her arms. "Well—don't."

The green bleeds back to his human hazel, and Cynthia lets a sigh of relief escape. Jason as human is bad enough. Wolfen is just plain dangerous.

"I already can't forgive myself," he confesses harshly.

"Why?"

Jason turns, and both of his fists come down on the wall. Cynthia yelps, retreating a step as her hands go to her chest, her heart bouncing around like a ping- pong ball.

They sure do a lot of wall repair here.

Jason turns away, speaking to the wall he just ruined, "Because of my clueless ass, Julia was taken, Kev was killed—eventually, you were turned."

"No, *God*—Jace!" Cynthia cries, moving behind him and putting her palms on his muscular back. "This is not on *you*." She slaps him lightly. "We didn't *know* this was even a part of our world."

Jason turns to face her. "But if I was always Singer, why didn't I have a gut instinct to protect Julia? Shouldn't I have known something?" His voice cracks, regret shattering the timbre into brittle glass.

"Remember the shooting, Jace?" Cynthia's eyes search his. "If *that* wasn't protecting her from that fuckwaffle teacher, I don't know what is."

Jason stares at her for half a minute, then he hugs her. "I *gotta* go, Cyn. I can't be here. I don't want anything bad to happen to Jules, but she's got *Scott*."

Cynthia pats his back then grips his T-shirt. "I know it's selfish, but I don't want you to leave. It's like breaking up the three musketeers or something."

Jason touches her cheek as he steps away. "Yeah. It is. But I'll hurt her worse if I stay. I can't stand that prick."

"Because he has Julia or something else?"

A rueful smile crosses his lips. "I don't have lofty principles. He's taking my wife, and that's all the reason I need to hate his stinking guts."

Cynthia can't respond to that. She understands. It's not reasonable, but it's real. And that's what matters to her.

She raises her eyes to meet his. "When?"

"I've got my shit packed. I'll say goodbye to Jules and get the hell out of here."

"What if there's, ya know, authorities hunting your butt?"

"Let 'em." He stuffs his hands in the pockets of his jeans but not before Cynthia catches sight of his scraped knuckles.

"There's nothing I can—" She wants to beg, to reason with him. There has to be a way.

"No."

She sees the determination on every tenacious line of his face. " 'Kay." Cynthia blows a stray hair out of her face, glancing down. "I'm sorry."

"Not your fault."

"It feels like it's all our faults."

Jason plows his fingers through his hair. "Maybe."

Cynthia jerks her face up.

Jason shrugs. "Feels like someone stole my life then gave it back to me like ground beef. And it's spoiled now."

"Gross analogy."

He lifts his shoulders. "Tell me I'm wrong?"

Cynthia shakes her head.

"Can't," she whispers.

Jason steps into her space and kisses her forehead, briefly cupping the back of her head. "Take care, Cyn."

She nods. There's no talking, too many tears and no decent words.

It sucks.

And that is all.

Julia

Her guilt is an endless swamp. Hot and rank, it washes around her legs, threatening to drown her with its smell and heat.

She knew he would come, but as Jason moves toward her, Julia still tenses in surprise.

"Hey," she calls out. For once, she's blissfully alone, yet she feels the separation from Scott like a weight.

Jason moves faster, and her eyes widen as he crashes into her and his arms snap around her smaller frame.

Julia opens her mouth to scream, and his lips smother hers as they smash into a wall in a tangle of arms and legs. His hands brace Julia before her head hits, his body pinning her against the exterior of the barn.

Jason kisses her fervently, desperately, and she opens her mouth to his. The kiss deepens, their tongues twining in a passion at once familiar, but now somehow wrong.

Though married, they're separate.

His assault on her mouth cools to pecking. Reluctantly he releases her. Jason grasps Julia's jaw, forcing her to meet his gaze.

Fear, sorrow, and adrenaline combine in a dizzying cocktail that surges through her and the tie she shares with Scott. "He's coming," she says.

Jason pulls a face of disdain. "Of course he would. Let him come."

Julia cups his face. A face she loves. A face she'll have to let go.

"Why, Julia?" he asks, slamming a palm into the wall next to her face, and she flinches.

She doesn't answer because Scott's pulling him off.

He hurls Jason ten feet, and he lands, his clothes bursting off his body as he morphs into wolfen.

Scott changes into his Combatant form in the time it takes her to expel the air from her lungs.

"No!" Julia screams.

Scott and Jason collide midair.

They land, and Julia steps between them. Strong hands latch on and fling her away, sending her airborne. Julia tries to work her telekinesis but fails as her emotional snare intensifies.

Scott catches her.

"Stay here," he growls, and Julia cringes when she sees his form. He whirls around, and there's empty space where Jason just was.

Vanished.

Julia doesn't know if it's forever. But it feels like it is.

Scott straightens from his crouch. The monster slowly melts back to human. Teeth like a saber tooth tiger's retract, talons as long as fingers slide to nails, his stature shortens, and his eyes stop glowing.

Julia takes a shuddering inhale and sits on her ass, dumping her face in her hands.

"That was awful," confessing the words as she fights sobbing and loses.

Scott doesn't agree, say he's sorry, or make excuses for himself or Jason. He scoops her off the ground and carries her to his bedroom.

Cyn puts a wet washcloth on Julia's forehead.

Bliss.

"That went well—*not.*"

Julia's eyes roll to meet Cyn's gaze. "Yeah. I felt like an ass."

"Jason's not really all there," Cyn says, tapping her temple. She plops down, perching at the side of Scott's bed.

"Wow, that sounds bad. Like I think Jace is nutso. I mean…" She sighs, wrapping her long hair in a fist and tossing it over her shoulder, "He's not crazy. He's just frustrated. But I think he finally made the right choice."

Julia's all talked out.

"He left so you *could* have a life, Jules. Jason left so he might, too."

"But he never came to terms with it—with us."

Cyn's eyes drift up to the ceiling then pierce Julia when they move back. "How could he? You're the one with the soul-meld—not him."

"With this thing"—Cyn swings her finger back and forth—"that you and Scott have—you have to move past memories. Jason doesn't have that buffer, the chemical things happening. He just has memories and devotion."

Julia dies a little inside at her words.

"And the fact that neither of us knew we were Singers. And the fact that he's a Were now. I mean, we're so far from being human anymore, it altered everything."

"I know," Julia concedes softly. Logically, with everything that's changed in their lives, there is zero chance that they, or their relationship, would have remained the same.

"I hate to say this, but you'll have to think about annulling the marriage."

Julia shakes her head, lacing her fingers tightly. "I can't. That would lead someone straight here." And on some level, she feels like shit for even contemplating it.

Cyn allows a smile. "Let Truman do it."

Julia crosses her arms. "Oh, yeah, that's so gonna work, Cyn. There's a manhunt gunning for Truman."

"Not so much, Jules. He's been gone awhile. Homer, Alaska, doesn't have the resources to look for a cop a year away from retirement age."

"A year away from retiring," Julia repeats in awe.

"I know, right?" She looks away, and color floods her cheeks. "He's like *so* not looking his age."

Julia scrutinizes her expression. "Do you kind of dig him?"

Cyn looks at her knotted hands. "Don't say."

Wow, Cyn is crushing on Truman.

"I thought we were talking about Jason here." Cyn huffs, swinging her leg.

"I think we've discussed him long enough. I don't—I can't deny I love him."

"But you're not *in* love."

Julia shakes her head. "I thought I was."

"Too much water under the bridge?" Cyn asks.

Julia gives her a defeated look.

"Too much blood."

Julia catches Scott's eye as he dips his head into the room.

He leaves without a word, allowing the women their grief for the past without him as an audience.

24

Slash

Slash loops his arm around Adrianna, drawing her against his body and kissing the top of her head. She smells of woods and him.

Slash likes it.

His wolf gives a joyous roll just beneath the thin layer of skin that makes Slash look human.

His animal is pleased by his choice of mate.

"You're all mushy and soft now, stud." Adrianna pokes him in the side. "Ooh, maybe not *too* soft."

She steps away and looks at his stomach, cocking her head. "You must have a twelve pack there. That's hot."

Slash raises his eyebrows, and he glances down at his flat stomach. "A what?"

She smacks him, and he catches her hand so quickly, she gasps softly. He flips her hand over and kisses the center of her palm.

She gives a contented sigh.

Slash could get so used to the noises she makes.

Adrianna blushes at the look he gives her.

"I thought you said you weren't the blushing virgin."

She looks up at him through her long eyelashes. "I'm not, anymore."

It's Slash's turn to feel a touch of embarrassment. He pulls her back to him, holding her close. "It was a precious gift you gave me."

"Slash," she says against his bare skin, "you don't have to be so serious all the time. Life's not so bad, y'know."

She is very young. Sometimes Slash forgets. He memorizes every line of her face and her every curve. Life is an ever-changing tide. When he navigated the current alone, it was manageable. Now there are two of them.

And someday, there may be a whelp. His chest swells at the thought of something he assumed would never be a part of his life. A thrill moves through him like an electrical current.

A twig snaps and Slash whirls, shoving Adrianna behind him.

His eyes skate across the woodland. All is in order, and he can vaguely see the dark outline of the Singer's mansion in the distance.

But Slash is Red, so he maintains his alert posture. He never dismisses his instincts. His eyes belie what his nose tells him is true. Adrianna's fingers grip his flanks, and he flexes in preparation for a change in form.

It is not necessary for a Were to change to full wolf except for that time the moon calls. A quick glance tells him the moon is half-gone. There is no wolf at the ready. And he would be horribly vulnerable when he changed back, leaving Adrianna unprotected.

No, determine the threat and go from there.

"Come out. I hear you," Slash announces loudly.

"Slash," Adrianna says. He can scent her fear as if it were his own. He shares it.

Slash didn't know fear before Adrianna. With a mate, it is part of the fabric of his thought process. Her welfare is a priority he can't deny even if he wanted to.

A large Were moves from a thick stand of trees and walks toward them gracefully. That is quite a feat, considering his size.

Instantly Slash intuits he's not from a nearby region.

Their nostrils flare as he approaches and both Were covertly scent the other.

Warily, the other Were circles Slash and Adrianna.

His eyes take her in as she stands behind Slash.

Slash growls low in his throat. "Do not look at her."

The strange Were cocks his head to the left as though considering it as a request. Of course it is not a request. Slash doesn't make those.

"She is yours?"

Odd phrasing.

Adrianna sucks in a breath. "Weiner," Adrianna mumbles quietly.

Slash ignores Adrianna's indignation. "She is my mate."

"Most recently, by the smell of it."

Slash stiffens, locking down his expression. "Voice your concern and business, Were."

"I am Tramack. And I believe you have something that belongs to me."

It's impossible for Slash to contain his confusion. His mind sprints through the possibilities and finally lands on the vague memory of two females arriving the day before. *Could that…?*

No. One is Lanarre. This Were is common, not a spot of either, Red—or Lanarre.

He *is* Alpha. And Slash senses he's a packmaster. He has that air of expected obedience about him.

Slash is obedient to no Were. "I don't have anything that belongs to you."

"I seek a female Alpha."

Slash shrugs, giving him nothing. "There are none but my mate, who you see here."

Tramack makes a show of scenting Adrianna from his distance of twenty feet.

Slash decides he doesn't like him. Of course, that's not atypical. A sudden thought occurs to Slash.

Where is Zeke?

"She is Alpha, but not who I seek."

His attention returns to Tramack. "I understand that."

"With whom do I speak?"

"Slash."

Tramack dramatically runs his eyes over Slash's scar.

"You know, you're a first-rate chode. Why don't you go hunt around for your chickie somewhere else," Adrianna comments.

Slash sighs. *She'll be the death of me.*

Tramack gives Adrianna a considering look. "You know"—his eyes flick to Slash's—"an insubordinate female from our pack would be handled before her behavior got out of hand, as it appears to have with your female."

Slash's patience thins. "She isn't from *your* pack."

"From which pack does she hail?"

Unease washes over Slash, and he squelches it before it can be scented. He deliberates whether he should answer or not. He decides against it. The less this Were knows, the better.

"Northwestern," Adrianna says.

Slash groans inside his skull.

Tramack gives a horrible smile of triumph that clenches Slash's guts. "Ah. That explains things."

Slash's frown turns to a scowl as his hands fall to hang at his sides. He doesn't like surprises. "Oh? Enlighten me."

"That packmaster is gone. The rumor mill's rife with stories of his death, along with his second's."

Tony.

And Manny. Slash had scented Lawrence and Emmanuel. They were buried beneath his feet. *How would Tramack know what Slash just confirmed?*

"We of the Western are tight sister dens with the North."

Chicken flesh rolls out like the red carpet across Slash's skin. Adrianna lays her face against his bare back, breathing in his scent.

Her uncharacteristic silence speaks for her fear. Slash hates that their tender moment together has been followed up by an unplanned meet with this power-hungry Tramack.

"If she is Northwestern, then automatically she is part of the Western if Lawrence is declared dead. You know this." Tramack tosses his hand out as though his words are a matter of course.

Slash's gut does a slow revolution. "I do."

"And you—you are not a part of the Northwestern." Tramack laughs.

Slash does not see the humor. All he can do is scent his female's fear mixed with misery behind him.

"You are Red. I'd know that taint anywhere."

Slash moves toward him and Adrianna grips him by the hips with slick palms, like an anchor at his back. "No, Slash. He's baiting you."

"Listen to the little woman, Slash," he jeers, "and enjoy what time you have with her before she is absorbed into my den." He thumps his chest.

"I'm not a 'little woman,' you neutered dog."

"Adrianna," Slash says like a slap, and she chokes back a sob.

Tramack gives Adrianna a thoughtful look. "I shall enjoy giving you a lesson in manners."

Slash shakes her hands off and dives against Tramack. They hit a wide trunk behind them with a crash. Slash lifts the other Were by the neck. "You will not touch her, look at her, or take her anywhere. There will be no lessons learned by your hand."

"You know Lycan law, Red. She cannot mate outside the pack. You thought yourself clever, that you could circumvent the law where it suited you."

Slash lowers Tramack to the ground, his anger clouding his scenting too late.

Four Were move out of the wood.

"Slash!" Adrianna yells.

Slash's face swivels to look at her. Alone and small, she's unprotected. "Stay there!" Slash roars.

Two of the Were split from their position, each one walking toward Adrianna.

Her quarter-change morphs to wolfen. Talons tremble at the tips of her fingers, and she whips them to her sides, the air whistling between the bony knives.

"Who's first to lose their teeny penis?" she growls, her talons clicking.

Slash loves her more than the moon.

Tessa

Tessa's been edgy all day. There was a huge ruckus when the Rare One and her human husband had a falling out, then he split. Her Singer soul-meld is now at her side, a bunch of misplaced Region Two Singers are here, and Tahlia's not happy with her.

And the two Singers she witnessed tossing the other Singer down a trapdoor chute in the middle of the hall... well, it feels like a fine time to go.

Tessa jogs down the hall to Tahlia's borrowed room, and with a quiet knock, she enters.

It scares the hell out of Tessa to see Tahlia packing.

"What is it?" she asks, looking from the bag to her exotic face.

Tahlia looks up from her packing. "I have a strange feeling."

That makes two of us.

"I'm already packed," Tessa admits.

"Do you—" Tessa sighs, giving her braid and irritated fling behind her shoulder. "I mean, I know you said you don't really own your life. But do you want to *not* wait for the Lanarre rescue committee, and just come with me?"

Tahlia bites her lip. After a full minute, she lifts her head. Her deep-blue eyes darken with a violet wash when her mood turns contemplative. "If he were wonderful, I would go with him."

"But that's the thing—you don't know."

Her curly hair bounces as she shakes her head. "I do not. He could be a tyrant. He could be arrogant."

A Lanarre who isn't arrogant. Tessa smirks at that.

"He could be hot."

They turn and the Rare One stands in the doorway.

Startled, Tessa says, "No offense, private conversation."

Julia spreads her hands away from her body inoffensively. "I understand. But if we're talking destiny here, I might have a clue." She gives a short laugh.

Tahlia nods. "I do appreciate your kindnesses."

"But…"

Tessa looks between them and is struck by their eyes—ancient eyes held prisoner inside their young faces. They've had to live too much for ones so young.

"But in this, I must choose," Tahlia says.

Julia glides through the door and walks to Tahlia. "You're brave. You survived your guardians being killed. You're in some kind of arranged marriage—"

"Not unlike your soul-meld."

Julia lips tip up. "Very *unlike* it. I feel love for Scott because it's actually in my blood." She puts a loose fist against her chest. "He's a part of me."

"Thank you, Julia." Tahlia leans forward to hug her.

Tessa watches the two women, who are so dissimilar, finding common ground.

"Stay," Julia implores, "The Lanarre guy—"

"Drek," Tahlia interrupts.

"Drek will show up. And you can be here, safe." Julia presses her hands against Tahlia's. "If you go, he'll have to look for you. And this guy Drek, he's not going to hurt you, is he?"

Shock spreads across Tahlia's features. "Absolutely not. A Lanarre would never hurt a female."

Julia looks down. When her face rises to meet Tahlia's eyes there's a wealth of sadness there. "Let me tell you about a Were named Anthony Laurent."

When Julia is done, Tessa thinks there's more to the story.

Tahlia sits down at the edge of the bed in defeat. "It was he. He was the Were who murdered my guardians. It could be no other."

This just gets worse and worse.

"I know it's rare for a Were to attack females, but this Were?" Julia shudders. "He also had demonic blood. He killed my people. He didn't spare anybody."

"He is dead?" Tahlia asks.

Julia nods.

Tahlia's eyes close, and a wrinkle of worry settles between them. Her eyes open slowly. "Yet…did he act under orders of another?"

"Yes, a demonic named Praile."

Tahlia works her lip between her teeth.

Julia leans forward. "We understand there's potential for retaliation. What are you thinking?"

Tessa's sense of foreboding kicks up a notch and her eyes bang around the room anxiously. "We need to go if we're going, Tahlia."

Tahlia nods. "My thoughts are only the legends I was raised with. The demonic are a race to be feared." She gives the smallest lift of her shoulders. "However, you are angelic here, so you have a powerful built-in opposition."

"And what about Drek?" Julia asks.

Tahlia gets a wistful look, gazing out a window without sight. Darkness has claimed the day.

"I'm not ready. I—" She gives Tessa a look. "I think I was just following what others thought was best for me. And now I know I can be something other than a mated Lanarre princess."

Her voice sounds uncertain.

"Are you sure that's what you want?" Julia's face looks pained. "What if he drops by and he's all kinds of amazing and kind and super handsome."

Tahlia's face breaks into a grin. "Well, he'll be worth being patient for. I'm just not ready, and Tessa wants a companion."

Julia gives Tessa a look that clearly says she's filled the girl's head with thoughts.

"Listen"—Tessa holds up her hands, glancing quickly at the window—"I'll check in after a couple of weeks once we're settled somewhere." She hikes her shoulders, sweeping a palm out in supplication. "And if Drak is here…."

Tahlia giggles. "Drek of the Lanarre, Tessa."

"Ah-huh. If Drek drops by, then by all means, let me know what your opinion is of him."

"I'll tell him I tried to talk sense into Tahlia."

Tahlia purses her lips. "I have an inordinate amount of sense."

Julia's face took on a sad cast. "I thought I did, too. Once."

Tessa's eyes swept the mostly empty room, landing on a duffel. "That it?"

Tahlia nods.

"I'll be back in a minute."

Tessa turns back from the doorway. "Thanks, Julia. For everything."

Julia stares at her with those unnerving eyes, like golden whiskey. "You're welcome."

It'd felt like home for a day.

Now the road would be home again.

⌒

Tessa tiptoes through the huge mansion, making a beeline for the kitchen.

She carefully packs two days' worth of food and loads a large hot-cold lunch bag full of food stuffs.

Tessa sets the thermos gently inside, careful not to crush the rest, and silently thanks Julia again for sharing.

The hairs at her nape suddenly lift, and Tessa curses herself for being too slow as a hand clamps over her mouth.

She kicks out, knocking the lunch sack over. A single orange pops out of the bag and bounces across the granite butcher block. It rolls all the way and lands against the wall. It ricochets off the wall and lands with a thunk as Tessa is drug off into the butler's pantry.

Her heels squeak against the wood floor as she quarter-changes and moves to lock teeth over the hand that grabs her.

"Do not."

That voice.

He jerks her over the pantry threshold and throws the door closed. He turns her in a blur of speed and slams her against the door. Tessa is momentarily stunned when her head thumps the wood.

It's the Singer, the lighter of the two who plunged the unconscious Victor into the hole.

Moon.

"I am here to kill you."

Tessa's never been a slave to her emotions. She's never cared about a male. She's been hunted, beaten, degraded and never, ever cherished.

In the middle of all that, she survived.

So when her heart races and her limbs go weak, she can't possibly grasp what this is about.

Smokey eyes gaze down into hers, and a light vapor rises off skin that has the faintest touch of red.

He smolders—his eyes, his skin…everything.

He is so hot, she can feel the heat emanating from his skin.

"So kill me," Tessa whispers.

She is weary.

She is finished with running. If she dies, then Tramack can never have her. In a bizarre way, Tessa wins.

He shakes his head, the ghost of a smile touching his lips. "No," he says, his fingers tightening against her throat. "I think not."

Tessa's confusion deepens.

He could take her down piece by piece. Somehow, this weird-looking Singer has the strength to outdo a quarter-changed female Alpha Were.

So why doesn't he?

"You saw what we did to the Singer."

I should have told Julia.

She licks her lips, and his eyes latch on to the movement.

"So, you're *not* going to kill me?" Tessa's thoughts spin.

He shakes his head. "I knew what you were to me the instant I scented you."

This guy's certifiable. I'll humor him.

His fingers loosen but don't drop from her flesh.

She hears herself asking, "Scented what?"

"My Redemptive."

Okay—really crazy.

He bends his much taller frame over her, but his hand doesn't let go. His thumb moves to her jaw and as his lips draw closer she tips her face up to give him better access.

I've obviously lost my mind, too.

This guy drug her inside a closet and told her he was going to kill her, and now he's going to kiss her.

And Tessa's going to let him.

Scorching heat sears through her lips as his land on hers. Tessa groans as if she's just awoken from a delicious sleep. Her every nerve ending fires. She doesn't realize her arms have encircled his neck until she molds herself against him like a second skin.

"So hot," she breathes against him.

He lifts her by the ass and buries himself against her.

"Ah," she moans and kisses him back. "Oh, moon, you feel right."

"As do you." Peck, lick, suck.

Tessa tries to pull back, and he sucks her lip deeper into his mouth. The sensation is wonderful, like heated bathwater concentrated into a single wonderful sip of sex on lips.

A surge of horrible disquiet flows over her and wakes Tessa from her sexual thrall.

She gasps.

"Who are you?"

She doesn't even know his name. And he is a Singer without a scent. He's no Singer.

An unknown male I'm making out with.

He allows Tessa to slide down the door but stops her momentum before she's a puddle of melted wax on the floor.

"They call me Lazarus."

"I mean—*what*—are you?"

He smiles, and Tessa is suddenly fascinated with a tongue so red it looks like it's on fire. *It was just in your mouth, dumbass.*

She swallows.

Lazarus brushes a hair away from her face and tucks it behind her ear. "I am demonic."

Tessa's hands slap the door behind her.

"Shh, do not fear me."

She nods. "Sure. Sounds like a great plan. I just made out with the devil, and you're telling me to calm down because things are so peachy. Right."

He ignores her words. "Do you know what a Redemptive is, Tessa of the Were?"

"It is my other half. Most demons do not have that potential. But demons of mixed parentage can be given this gift." His eyes skip away from hers to return a heartbeat later.

"I'm a Were. You're a demon." She points from her to him. "It's not a match made in—"

He presses a finger to her lips, and Tessa watches the light steam rise and evaporate from his skin.

Her throat feels tight.

"None of those words, Tessa."

"Okay," she squeaks, her eyes flitting to where his hands are. "It's been ah—great—to make—I mean—meet you, but now it's time to go."

Lazarus shakes his head again. "You are my only chance. If I take you as my bride, I will never have to return to Hades and suffer under the Master again. We are meant to be together. Only my Redemptive can free me from the bonds of hell."

Tessa finds air isn't reaching her lungs. "What about your partner or whatever?"

He scowls, and Tessa finds her out.

"He won't like it. You just let me go, and then everything will be okay. You can keep on being evil and that, and I'll keep on…"

What will she keep on doing?

Oh, yeah. Running.

Lazarus moves in tight against her body. "I cannot force the Redemptive. She must be willing."

His hands slides behind her neck, and she groans against his touch. She's lost to it.

So lost.

What is wrong with me?

"Do you not feel the pull?"

Tessa does, right between her legs.

"Yes," she admits. "But it's not enough. I mean, you're not even a Were? I can't just up and go with you."

Tessa gets an image of a future whelp. A hotdog comes to mind. She shivers.

This isn't going to work. Tessa needs space—right now.

She shoves him, and he steps away, every hot inch. His six feet four-ish of hardened muscle is scentless but oh-so fragrant anyway.

When her gaze reaches his lips, Lazarus twists them into what she guesses is his version of a smile. His gray eyes storm at her.

His light-blond hair begs for her fingers.

She blushes hard when she thinks of the other things.

"I can scent your arousal, Tessa."

She backs up a step.

Too dangerous. Just too everything.

"I can't do this, sorry. You're so tempting. Like a pile of chocolates that'll never make me fat."

"I won't stop," Lazarus says.

Tessa blindly finds the doorknob behind her then opens the door. "Stop what?"

"Wanting you." He grabs the door as she tries to swing it shut between them.

"Ever," his deep voice rumbles.

She jerks it closed and sprints away.

25

Scott

Scott would be happier without the soul-meld. He has no doubt. Right now, things suck.

His dad is dead. Most of Region One is dead.

And Julia's emotions constantly batter him. He can't blame her. Her selfish asshole of a husband dumps his baggage at her doorstep to figure out while every stinking supe demands guidance from a twenty-two-year-old woman.

His heart aches where it never did before.

Scott figures there's one asshole down and a few more to go. He strides to the barn. Julia should be back there now.

He knows she is. He can feel her like a beacon inside his body. She dealt with Tahlia and Tessa while he broke the shitty news of what happened in the seventy-two hours his siblings were locked up in the bunker.

And Victor from Two? Where the hell did he run off to?
Scott is pissed. He saves who he can, rises from the ashes
with Scott's sister and brother, then disappears. *Not cool.*
Scott needs his stuck-up ass.

Lucius and he were separated after the torture he
escaped from. The other Combatants were killed in the
battle of the demonic. And Julia has a demon spore making her sick.

The trouble never stops.

But after holding Jen while she cried on him for an
hour, Scott is ready for the healing the soul-meld will provide him. If he can just lay hands on Julia, all will be well,
as his father would have said.

Scott pinches the bridge of his nose. Even smart-ass
Michael, when faced with one of his junky suckers, couldn't
bear to pop one in his cocky mouth.

They're in shock, he tells himself.

That's all well and good, but for two guys who wear
their sister's grief on their shirt, logic and explanations just
don't fucking cut it.

If he can get Tharell and his own evolving bio-mom
out of here, so much the better.

Speak of the devil.

Tharell comes into view, along with Brynn, Delilah,
Domiatri and Jacqueline.

Now that he thinks of it, Scott isn't quick to shake his
prejudice against vamps. The only good vamp is a dead
vamp. At least he and Caldwell agree on that.

Or they did.

That powder keg is gone now.

He feels the bond grow snug with each step he takes toward Julia.

Julia's head turns, and his body weeps to connect with hers. As though he's moving through quicksand, each step he takes is heavier than the last. She moves to meet him.

They collide softly. She whimpers against his chest. "It's so hard."

"Yeah," Scott agrees, touching her everywhere and scenting deeply of her hair as Julia molds her body to his. Seconds pass into a minute while everything rights itself.

His body grows stronger, and the fog of lethargy clears from his mind. All his senses come online and sharpen. Scott can think again.

"We can't be away from each other that long," Julia says with a shaky exhale.

"Feel better?" he asks, looking down at her.

She nods. "Much."

Scott looks around him, and the others stand silently.

"You're going?" he asks Jacqueline.

"Don't sound so happy, my son," Jacqueline says.

Scott threads his large hand through Julia's smaller one and she stands at his side. "I've had enough bullshit and strife to last two lifetimes. I'm good with the fey going back where they belong, and no offense—I don't think vamps for hire appeals much either."

"No offense taken, Singer." Brynn hisses, his fangs sprouting like dual razors.

"Right," Scott drawls.

"Scott," Julia says in a low voice. "Let's just let them go, and when thing settles and hell's not chasing our butts, we can make good on the promise."

Scott turns to Julia, his gaze intent on hers. "There might not be enough Singers to make good on that exchange, Julia."

She bites her lips, and Scott smooths them with a tender finger. "No, Julia." He shakes his head and addresses Tharell and Domi. "You guys"—he swings his finger between the two—"there will be some Singers who want to live in faerie." For the life of him, Scott can't come up with a single name. "But I don't know when, or who."

"Do not break a promise to the fey, Scott," Tharell warns.

Scott moves to the Sidhe warrior. "I'm well aware of the promise Julia made. But you're a traitor. And as such, I feel I'm being pretty fucking charitable to honor anything."

"Scott."

He turns to his mother, whose belly is swollen with Domi's child. He can't wrap his head around it all, so he doesn't bother.

"It's a promise to faerie, not Tharell. Faerie sends justice to oathbreakers."

"We won't break our promise."

Domi steps forward. "See that you do not. Make haste in an alliance between the fey and the Singers. Quickly."

Scott feels Julia's fear, and he wants to knock some rainbow heads together. But he's not going to pull a Caldwell. He's going to think things through. *What's best for Julia. Them. The Singers.*

Fuck the fey. Yet…Scott is old enough to understand the consequence of ignoring magic set in motion.

Instead of voicing his heated thoughts, he says, "We'll be in touch."

Julia squeezes his hand and he pulls her against him.

Jacqueline moves from Domi as his hand reluctantly slides down her arm. She stands before him and for the first time Scott looks at her, really looks at her.

She *has* changed. Julia is right. Her eyes no longer hold that vacant indifference. It has been replaced with cautious hope.

Jacqueline doesn't move to take his hands, but Julia elbows him, and he feels what she feels for Jacqueline—forgiveness.

He can't hate her anymore if Julia doesn't. And she *is* his family.

Scott doesn't know what family they will all end up being to him but when he looks over at Delilah, she is already making her way to him.

Julia steps away so he can embrace his mother and sister.

A small tear in his psyche begins to mend as his eyes hunt and find Julia.

She smiles, and it lights him from within.

And Scott knows everything will be all right.

Praile

Praile is as mad as he's ever been. *Where in Hades is Lazarus?* Praile has sighted the High One with the one who carries the blood babe. *And Lazarus is where?*

Holding his hot dick while he takes a sizzling piss?

Praile writhes with his anger.

He gave Lazarus explicit instructions to meet with him in this exact spot. Then they would take the women at one time. The High One had not divulged her scheme to return the Sidhe and the others to faerie.

It's a perfect situation for Praile, though. The fewer supernaturals to deal with, the better. However, killing the High One would be tricky.

She has a formidable arsenal at her disposal. Hopefully, she isn't fully aware of all the strengths she possesses.

And she and her soul-meld are fools. If they have not consummated their relationship by coming together, she is vulnerable. Praile and Lazarus have not been at the compound long enough to understand the entire story, but he understands her human marriage has delayed her consummation with the soul-meld.

Praile makes a disgusted noise. *Some kind of illogical, emotion-based nonsense.* This gives Praile the advantage.

Julia would be invincible if the soul-meld were consummated.

It should be an impenetrable golden circle.

Praile would find the chink in her unfinished armor. Praile leaks vapor then clenches his teeth until it subsides. He hates the human shell.

It is as ugly as sin.

The thought makes his face break into a grin.

Tessa

Tessa drags both duffels and settles them into the back of a borrowed SUV. It's as old as hell but runs true.

Well, that's what one of the Region Two Singers said.

He palms the keys in her hand and smiles. "Julia says to get it back when you come back."

Tessa is so unaccustomed to kindness that she blinks back tears.

Tahlia squeezes her arm. Their eyes meet, and Tessa glances away before revealing too much.

Tessa thinks of Lazarus and his threat. She shivers, despite feeling the heat of him against her.

Then, with a shudder, she remembers who chases her.

She stiffens her spine. *Don't be a baby, Tessa. Get your ass in gear.* She can't be with a demonic, no matter how amazing that interlude was back there.

She can't stay here and endanger the Singers, because sadistic Tramack is chasing her.

She glances at Tahlia, who slides into the car. And she can't leave a young woman barely out of whelp for a mystery match.

Tessa closes the back of the late-70s Chevy Suburban and makes her way toward the front.

"Tessa," a low voice commands from the woods, and on reflex, she looks up.

Tramack smiles.

Two Were drag a badly beaten Were between them. Shackled in silver, he can barely open his eyes.

The sight of the female takes her breath away. Her talons are broken, many at the base, and one eye is swollen shut. A third Were carries her in his arms.

She doesn't move.

Tessa scents they're alive. She also has a vague recollection of meeting them and doesn't know what happened.

What Tessa knows is she's seen so much worse than this.

The female will survive.

I'm so sorry, she whispers in her mind. If she helps, Tramack will win.

She will be his victim, along with the Were he's already captured.

Tessa glances at Tahlia, and the girl turns the keys in the ignition. The engine roars to life, and Tessa grasps the handle.

Tramack bellows, charging toward her, and Tessa whimpers. A body is suddenly pressing behind her, a hand covering her own.

Light-red flesh warms her hand, making the metal too hot to touch, and Tessa snatches her hand back as strong arms hold her still as Tramack bears down on her. She knows the embrace. Her soul recognizes him as though she's been waiting her entire life to be held by him.

Lazarus.

She's not scared.

For the first time, Tessa feels safe.

26

Julia

*J*ulia's arm encircles Scott's waist, and she lays her head on his bicep.

They watch the group walk away.

"You're relieved," Julia says.

"Yeah, can't you feel it?"

She nods against him, and he closes his hand around the back of her head. He would glue her to him if he could.

I heard that.

Scott deliberately inserts the image of super glue, and she giggles.

He strokes her hair.

They have a minute of peace before the nasty wound inside Julia begins to pulse and throb.

"What is that?" Scott asks.

Julia groans, her hand going to her stomach. "It's that demon's blood."

"Oh, babe," Scott says, kissing her mouth. "We'll figure that out."

Gravel crunching under a footstep causes them to look up. Julia forces a smile through the pain. "Hi, Peter," she says.

"Hey," Scott says, but Julia feels a mild trepidation leaking from him. He's so paranoid. The guards actually found more Region Two survivors, and all Scott can think of is finding Victor so he can verify their identities. Julia's mind gets fuzzy as the demonic blood surges as though it's a magnet set on something outside her body.

"Where's the other guy?" Julia asks. She snaps her fingers with a small grimace as the pain intensifies. She ignores it. "Laz?"

Peter smiles, and hers falters. There's something there.

Julia's skin begins to crawl as though a million biting insects are swarming over her flesh.

"Julia!" Scott yells from somewhere far away.

Peter strolls slowly to her and she's slipping. She falls to the ground and Scott is writhing on the floor.

Why is he half-changed into Combatant form?

There'd have to be a direct threat to her life.

Peter grins. His teeth are black.

Julia screams.

Then she screams louder when the cloak of his humanity falls away, and his true form stands before her.

"Tony did well after all."

"Scott," Julia whispers.

She'd asked for privacy to say goodbye to the fey.

"Julia!" Scott crawls to her, his veins pulsing gold and silver. His skin smolders.

As does Peter's. *Or whoever he is.*

He sinks down beside her.

Julia cringes, trying to scrape together her powers, but nothing comes.

The demon places the flat of his palm on her stomach, and pure agony surges through her. It feels like he's commanding her spine to come through her stomach, and she opens her mouth to scream. No sound comes out. The pain is so total, so awful that there is no breath to wail.

She contorts, her back arching.

"I am Praile. And you will die, High One. And then I will capture the mother of the blood babe."

Scott crawls closer.

"Jacqueline," Julia instantly squeezes through her pain-addled brain.

Praile's inky brows tug together.

"No, part-demonic and fey, part-vampire and angelic, enemies of blood, and born of strife."

Julia's head goes in the direction of where the party of fey traveled.

Ice slides up her spine.

Delilah!

Her attention snaps back to Praile as a gruesome tail settles above his head. His palm is fire against her flesh, and the light of her blood is blinding.

But the spore of the demonic has allowed entry to degrade her body, she realizes.

The ball at the end of his tail is spiked. It whips above his head more quickly than she can track, and he brings it down just as he lifts his palms.

Her eyes meet Scott's as he takes her hand.

A club swings through the air, whistling, then hammers into the ribcage of the demon bent on ending her. Praile staggers back.

Spinning green discs meet her gaze, and she can't move.

Jason's wolfen form bends and scoops her into his arms. He reaches behind him and grabs a semi-conscious Scott. He drags the other man behind him as he jogs toward the mansion.

Scott's head bounces over the terrain and Julia lays like a bag of rocks as Jason makes his way into the house.

He sets Julia down gently and releases Scott, who groans when his head hits the carpet. Jason throws the carpet off, and Julia watches him enter a series of numbers into a door in the floor. Air hisses, and Jason's long fingers tear open the top.

Victor's head is out in an instant.

Jason turns and hands Julia to Victor, who takes her below.

Next Scott tumbles inside, and Victor catches him badly, the two of them rolling into a pile on the cold floor.

Julia drags herself to the bottom of the ladder and looks up to meet Jason's eyes.

"I love you, Julia."

She opens her mouth.

Praile appears behind him, his tail swings high, and the mallet connects with Jason's head, shattering his skull as she watches.

Julia releases the last rung and falls to the floor.

Jason loses his hold on the hatch, and it closes as Praile's hands frantically claw at the metal for purchase and miss.

Julia escapes in the only way she knows how, an unconsciousness of necessity sweeps over her, and she falls into an unnatural sleep of survival.

The End

Never *miss a new release, copy and paste the link below:*

bit.ly/NEWS-TRB

Read on *for an exciting sample chapter from a TRB/Marata Eros sexy paranormal urban fantasy serial....*

Vampire

ALPHA CLAIM 1

MARATA EROS

NEW YORK TIMES & USA TODAY BESTSELLING AUTHOR

TAMARA ROSE BLODGETT

VAMPIRE: ALPHA CLAIM 1
a Brief-Bites novelette
Copyright © 2014-15 Marata Eros
Copyright © 2014-15 Tamara Rose Blodgett

Narah Adrienne is a bounty enforcer in the near future. She runs the seedy side of her game, capturing criminals too dangerous for the local law enforcement. Using unorthodox methods, she finds herself in the crosshairs of the Magistrate for too many allowable kills for the quarter.

And her head hurts like hell.

Aeslin is part of an elite vampire squad of Turners. A rare sect of vampire scouts who possess the ability to find women with enough undead blood to be turned into full vampire. As the numbers of supernaturals dwindle, it is the hope of the Nobles that extinction can be a thing of the past with female hybrids.

In a race against time and common enemies, can Aeslin find the one female who is meant to be turned and also his parallel soul? Or will the fabled carrot the Nobles dangle turn out to be a lie perpetuated by desperation?

1

Narah

My legs are kicked up on the desk, the toes of my left combat boot stacked on the heel of my right. I lean my feet a couple of inches to the left and look at my boss.

Kinda wish I hadn't.

The tongue-lashing was going to be brutal, and not the fun kind. I just barely hold back a snort of self-serving comedy.

"Narah," Casper leans into the desk, edging a butt cheek on the only part not covered by my assortment of shit. My eyebrow cocks. Perturbed doesn't cover it. If I wanted a butt on my desk, I'd ask.

"What?" I bark with anticipation.

A vein in Casper's forehead throbs and I dial it back some. No need to bring the guy to heart failure.

"What?" I repeat more good-naturedly, though both of us know I'm nothing of the sort.

He sighs, scrubbing a palm over his face. Hair almost as white as swan feathers glows under the LED lighting in my tiny office, and his glacial eyes tighten, fighting for a view of my face over the top of my boot.

I jack my feet down and stuff them underneath my desk. My fingers itch to go to my smart phone. Anything to not commit to this conversation.

"You know we appreciate your skill set."

Blah, blah, stinking-blah.

"But we can't have you pulling firearms on all your bounties."

My bottom lip pops out in a pout. "It was a very small gun, Casper." I put my index and thumb almost touching.

"Using manstopper ammunition?"

He might have a small point.

"Outlawed in 1898," Casper adds.

I shrug a bare shoulder, my tank top skin-tight against my small frame. I find loose clothes are handles to make a bludgeon against me easier. I nail the targets but if there's nothing for them to grab onto, so much the better.

"I like antique weaponry and ammunition," I say with deliberate nonchalance.

"Really?" Casper says and I wince at the sound of his voice. "Let's run down the list of target fatalities."

Hmmm.

"Target 103, lethal stabbing."

I lean back in my chair and cock my neck back, staring at the dingy ceiling. A water stain has spread out from the center in a pattern of copper lines that somehow resemble a flower opening.

It's sort of like watching clouds outside, but inside.

"Narah!"

I sigh, answering the ceiling. "Yeah."

"Target 424, beheading."

Yeah, that'd been messy.

"Again, I was in fear for my life," I say, not sounding defensive.

At. All.

"Thirteen times?" Casper asks softly.

My chin snaps down and I meet his eyes. Mine are big and golden hazel like a cat's, and that's why I hide them behind my aviator shades. The sun hurts like hell. I've always been sensitive to sunlight.

I shrug. It'll get me nowhere to fight with Casper. Who has the nickname in the office of, The Ghost. No one says it to his face though. I fight a snicker.

"We are the last profession for use of lethal force, you know. It's not goddamned 2015, when everyone thought all physical force was necessary in some capacity."

I'm in the wrong era, I muse with regret.

"We are the last stand against the criminals of our time. When the police can't nail them, then it's up to us. But Narah," Casper scrubs his head, his crewcut bristling from the contact, "we can't have you killing all the targets. They must be brought to justice."

And of course, if I kill a target, Casper doesn't get credits. That's what this is *really* about. I bring in the most targets in our office. I get results and he gets credits for my hard work.

We stare at each other. I won't break and Casper knows it. "You're the finest bounty hunter we have. Your instincts are uncanny, and you never let being a woman get in your way…"

I lunge to my feet and Casper jerks to his, eyeing me warily.

Good, my desk is finally free of his ass.

"Nothing about me being a woman comes into play here."

Casper shoots out an exhale like a cannon. "Everything about it matters. You're smaller, you're vulnerable to things a man could never be."

Rape is the clear inference.

"You think a man can't be raped?" I bark out a laugh. "You think that my looks don't disarm. They do, Cas." My eyes laser down on him and his shift away. "You know I'm a proficient, Level Ten."

"Nothing to sneeze at," he concedes and opens his mouth to add more, perhaps dig his grave a little deeper.

I raise my palm. *Nothing to sneeze at.* I can feel a royal conniption fit brewing. "No. If I've killed while gunning for a target," Casper frowns at my wording which causes me to grin, "then they needed dying. Period."

Casper walks to my office door. "I'm sorry, Narah, I've done what I could, but the law states that there can't be more than ten sanctions in one quarter. You have thirteen. I got the bonus three waived." He whips his palm in the air like he's performing a magic trick. "Now you'll have to go before the magistrate."

Fuck. They'd plug me a second ass after a first class reaming. If—*if* I could even bounty again.

I jerk my leather jacket off the back of my chair and sling it on. A bright headache, a new friend of mine of late, settles into my temples with zeal. I press my fingers against my head.

I hate not having a target. The chase is the one thing that makes my life worth living. No longer an outcast—always in the game.

Now the rules are being threatened.

And all I want to do is play.

2

Aeslin

*E*dan jerks a thumb my way, throwing a towel I deftly catch. I dab at the sweat running like a river from my scalp and making its way to the waistband of my work out gear.

"Corcoran's asking for you."

I look at him, narrowing my eyes.

"Hey man, don't kill the messenger," Edan's hands spread away from his body.

He'd look so much more innocent if he had even one spot of bare skin. Edan's tatted from head to toe. Well... that's not entirely accurate. Don't think his feet hold the tats of our species. Or his face.

Turners are required to be marked.

It's grounds for immediate execution to civilian vampires if they touch us. After all, we're the only savior of our dying race. They can't miss our marks. In the human world, tattoos no longer stand out. We hide in plain sight now.

I flick irritated eyes to him. "I'm on leave, Edan."

He shrugs. "You know the drill. If a female comes on the radar, we're all on alert."

I throw the damp towel in the soiled laundry hamper. I'm bone tired. Not physically—mentally. So many scouting expeditions and coming up empty handed has taken its toll. I rub a hand on my nape, trying to make a raw spot. "I've worked a solid quarter—nothing."

My eyes meet his. Edan's looks are unusual for a Turner. Most of the sub-sect of vampire Turners possess dark coloring. Our only unified feature are silver eyes. Edan's are amber. Some kind of genetic throw back. My own hair is a deep chestnut, more red than what is considered fashionable. And if we want to enjoy female vampire company, it matters. They're few and far between. If they can't be our mates, it's only for release. And that's become an empty vessel.

"But what if we have a live one?"

I smirk at his words. "You mean undead, right?"

Edan throws up his hands. He's muscled, like the rest of us. Mandatory training makes our bodies at battle readiness. Last month we'd just missed a female by minutes.

She'd been sterilized. Technically, it'd been on our watch.

The loss had brought the entire team down and morale had not recovered.

Edan spoke my thoughts, "We need this, Aeslin. We need a female. They're so vulnerable to the Hunters…"

I toss my palm up. "We've been over this. It's a race against them. And they got to that female first." I see guilt on his face and know mine looks the same.

"Then why can't you see that every lead should be followed?"

Tired of fucking losing, that's why. Or just tired.

My eyes feel like they're on fire when I glare at Edan, a Turner I've fought shoulder to shoulder beside. "You don't think it haunts my fucking every thought that she could have belonged to one of us?"

"Does it?" Edan asks in soft disbelief.

"Yes," I hiss defensively.

"Then join us."

I don't want another dead end. Another disappointment. "I'm not rested."

"So when has that ever mattered?" he asks.

Since that female was lost, I think but don't say.

Corcoran stands at the window when I walk into his office and shut the door.

He doesn't turn.

Corcoran is a Noble.

A politically correct word for being in charge of the Turners. But he became a Noble the hard way, having been a Turner first and struggling through the ranks to prove himself invaluable to the cause. Now he rules over the Turners of our region with an iron fist.

Hell, in his day, there was a female turned every month. Now we were lucky to turn one a quarter. However, there was one biological advantage. A human female with vampire blood once turned, was always meant for her biological other half. Lucky bastard. It meant offspring.

A chance at happiness.

With Hunters killing off every vampire they could, our numbers continued to dwindle. In the last half-century, one in two females who possessed enough of the blood of our kind had been sterilized before they could be turned, negating their vampire ancestry and the ability to have children.

A Turners' goals were two-fold. Find the hybrid vampire females before the Hunters did, and determine how they were setting their sights on the rare females.

Easier said than done.

"Aeslin," Corcoran said as greeting.

I remain silent.

Corcoran turns, eyeing me up. "You look rested." He sounds hopeful. We both know I've had only four days respite.

I need a month.

I haven't taken enough blood, had enough sex, slept inside the ground as I should. A lot of *have nots* on the short list of my exhaustion.

I lift my shoulders in an answer that isn't one. It will do no good to rehash the discussion I had with Edan.

Corcoran says something under his breath. It sounds suspiciously like a curse.

"You're the best I have, Aeslin," he says quietly.

"Let Edan take it. Hell—Jaryn could…"

His gaze darkens. Eyes not the common light gray of the Turner are pewter in a face devoid of emotions. Corcoran's gaze is a coming storm.

"I need you on this."

That's just what Edan said. "I mean no disrespect…"

"Yes, you do," he says with the barest bit of humor.

My lips thin. "Yes."

"She's a Turn, Aeslin. I know it." Corcoran closes his fingers into a fist.

My breath leaks out of me in defeat. "Okay."

I simply don't believe anymore. There's been so many dry runs I can't remember the last one that wasn't.

"She's sending out pheromones like a distress signal."

"Who called it?"

His face closes down. "Torin."

Corcoran and Torin don't see eye-to-eye. I say nothing, waiting. I'm not political and won't immerse myself in it now.

Corcoran slams a fist against the wall that bisects the bulletproof windows. "She's bounty."

His frustration gets my attention. Hell, her occupation stalls me and I unlace my fingers and straighten my posture. "What?"

"Damn," he grits through his teeth, knowing full-well the risks of this acquisition.

I tell him anyway. "Too high profile," I state, hands going to my hips.

"She's manifesting."

Dammit.

"Is Torin sure she's a Turn?"

Corcoran exhales in a rush, taking a rough palm down his face, nodding.

I suck in a deep breath. "I'll do it."

Corcoran looks relieved. "You know the risk?"

Hell yes. But another sterilized female? That we don't need. Can't stand.

"Yes," I answer.

If Torin's got a bead on her, then so do the Hunters.

The thought of a female out there and vulnerable tightens my guts. This is the part of my job I hate. However small, the emotion is there in my suppressed emotional makeup. The hardest to squelch, the most damning.

Hope.

Acknowledgments

It's been since March 31, 2011, when my first book, Death Whispers, was published. I'd like to take this opportunity to thank each and every one of my readers. Without you, I would not have an audience for my work. Your support, recommendations, encouragement, and critical feedback have allowed my improvement as a writer and as a human being. Ironically, words are inadequate for expressing the depth of my gratitude. Please know how much your support has meant and will continue to mean in the future.

Thank you from the bottom of my heart.

Dear Ones:
Danny
Cameren: Without you, there would be no books.

Thank you:

My *Readers*

Special thanks to the following: *Beth Dean Hoover, Dii, Lori* and *Shana B.* for all your help and support.

More books from Tamara Rose Blodgett:

BLOG: Tamara Rose Blodgett

THE DEATH SERIES
(Dark dystopian fantasy):

Death Whispers
Death Speaks
Death Inception
Death Screams
Death Weeps
Unrequited Death
The Death Bundle, books 1-3
For the Love of Death
Death Blinks- 2015

THE SAVAGE SERIES
(Dark post-apocalyptic steampunk paranormal romance):

The Pearl Savage
The Savage Blood
The Savage Principle
The Savage Vengeance
The Savage Protector

The Savage Dream
The Dark Savage 6.1
The Dark Savage 6.2 (May 29, 2015)
Savage Bundle, Books 1-3

THE BLOOD SERIES
(Dark paranormal romance):

Blood Singers
Blood Song
Blood Chosen
Blood Reign
Angelic Blood

THE REFLECTION SERIES

(Dark dystopian fantasy):

The Reflective (The Reflection Series, #1)
The Reflective Cause- July 3, 2015

Books under the pen name, Marata Eros:

THE DRUID SERIES:

Reapers

Bled

Harvest

Sow

Seed

Plow

Thresher

Exotic

The Druid Breeders

Baird

Seraphina 9.5-2015

THE SIREN SERIES:

Ember

Constantine

Brandon

Alicia 3.5-2015

THE DEMON SERIES:

Brolach

Ruby 1.5- 2015

THE TOKEN SERIAL:

The Token
The Token 2
The Token 3
The Token 4
The Token 5
The Token 6
The Token 7: Thorn
The Token 8: Kiki
The Token 9: Chet Sinclair

DARK ROMANTIC SUSPENSE:

A Terrible Love
A Brutal Tenderness
The Darkest Joy
In Broken Love

ALPHA CLAIM SERIES:

Brief-Bites novelettes

Vampire 1-6
Lycan
Demonic
Angelic
Hunter
Harborer

THE DARA NICHOLS SERIES, 1-8:

A Hard Lesson
To Protect and Service
The 13th Floor
The Boardroom
The Four Whoresmen
The Masquerader's Balls
The Ball Player
The Cock Tale

THE ZOE SCOTT SERIES 1-8:

Smoldering Wet
Cold Fire
Internal Combustion
Back Draft
Charged Hose
Pike Pole
Point of Ignition
Boiling Over
The Zoe Scott Series, 1-8

BLOG: marataeroseroticaauthor.blogspot.com

About the Author

Tamara Rose Blodgett is the author of over fifty titles, including her *New York Times* bestselling novel, *A Terrible Love*, and the international bestselling TOKEN serial, written under the pen name Marata Eros. Tamara writes a variety of dark fiction in the genres of erotica, fantasy, romance, suspense and sci-fi. She lives in South Dakota with her family and enjoys interacting with her readers.

Connect with Tamara:
Never miss a new release:

SUBSCRIBE: http://tinyurl.com/
TamaraRoseBlodgettNewsletter

BLOG: http://tamararoseblodgett.blogspot.com/

TWITTER: @TroseBlodgett

FACEBOOK: http://tinyurl.com/TamaraRoseBlodgettFB

Made in the USA
Monee, IL
12 April 2021

65535000R00184